Red's Untold Tale

ONCE UPON A TIME
Red's Untold Tale

By **Wendy Toliver**

Based on the ABC Television series created by
Edward Kitsis & Adam Horowitz

KINGSWELL TEEN

Los Angeles • New York

Copyright *Once Upon a Time* © 2015 ABC Studios. All Rights Reserved.

Published by Kingswell Teen, an imprint of Disney Book Group. No part of this book may be reproduced or transmitted in any form or by any means, electronic or mechanical, including photocopying, recording, or by any information storage and retrieval system, without written permission from the publisher.

For information address Kingswell Teen,
1200 Grand Central Avenue, Glendale, California 91201.

Editorial Director: Wendy Lefkon
Executive Editor: Laura Hopper
Cover designed by Julie Stephens

Printed in the United States of America
First Paperback Edition, May 2018
10 9 8 7 6 5 4 3 2 1

FAC-020093-18082

ISBN 978-1-368-02609-3

www.disneybooks.com

SUSTAINABLE FORESTRY INITIATIVE   Certified Sourcing
www.sfiprogram.org
SFI-00993

THIS LABEL APPLIES TO TEXT STOCK

This book is dedicated to
the fans of *Once Upon a Time*

ONCE UPON A TIME

Red's Untold Tale

By Wendy Toliver

One

I'm not afraid because I sense that I'm not alone. I don't see anyone, but I hear a familiar voice. Though it sounds like it's coming from far, far away, being carried by the wind, I hear it clearly. The voice reminds me to breathe. I inhale, and the darkness enters my lungs, spreading throughout my body, filling me with energy.

Power.

Hunger.

With outstretched arms, I reach higher and higher. Between the shadows, splinters of light glisten just out of my grasp—morphing into thousands of fireflies caught in a tornado. I kick and claw my way up, through layers of dirt, roots, grasses, tree trunks, branches, twigs, leaves.

Then—nothing but air.

The wind blows through my hair as I throw my head back and blink in the sudden brightness. The full moon illuminates the land, and I'm filled with reverence and warmth.

Saturday, May 12

I woke up in a sweat and kicked off my covers. The quilts and fur pelts tumbled to the floor, landing in a heap. Warm sunlight poured through my bedroom window, and outside, the rooster crowed hoarsely. Blinking and stretching away my drowsiness, I realized I'd had one of my dreams last night, and that meant Wolfstime was coming.

Three and a half years ago, when I turned thirteen, I started having the Wolfstime dreams. Though each was different, they always began in complete darkness. It wasn't ordinary darkness—say, a night without moon or stars, or the deepest cave, or how I imagined it looked at the very bottom of a well. It was much, much darker than that. Like I was completely submerged in a sea of tar.

I never told anybody about my dreams—not Vicar Clemmons, not my friend Peter, not the girls at school, and most certainly not Granny. I knew that the dreams were strange, which meant *I* was strange, and that was the last thing I wanted people to think. Besides, my dreams felt sacred, like they were a secret part of me—and it was up to me to put the pieces together and somehow make sense of the bizarre images, sounds, and emotions.

Before my grandmother could poke her nose in and scold me for having slept in nothing but my undergarments again, I wiggled into my blouse, bodice, and skirt and ventured through the living room into the kitchen.

"Hello? Granny, where are you?"

To get a head start on the day's baking, my grandmother usually awakened well before me and even before the rooster—which was a good thing because I hated to imagine how grumpy she was before getting a couple cups of coffee in her. Not bothering to cover my yawn, I filled the pot with water and lit a fire below it.

Granny's snores thundered through the cottage, and I shook my head. She said it was unladylike to sleep in nothing but one's undergarments, yet I couldn't think of anything more unladylike than snoring. Well, maybe scratching oneself in public. Or growing a beard. Still, it sounded like a mean ole grizzly was hibernating in Granny's bedroom.

I pondered waking her up but decided against it. Tonight was Peter's birthday party, and I wanted to bake a cake for him—and having the kitchen all to myself was a rare and beautiful thing. Just think: I could put whatever I pleased in a bowl and mix it all up without having her breathing down my neck. Besides, the little kitchen didn't seem nearly as crammed without Granny.

The bowls, plates, and cups were stacked neatly in the pale yellow cabinets. A pitcher and a skillet sat on the countertop where they'd dried overnight, and behind them, jars of spices, flour, and sugar were lined up against the wall. Sunlight shone through the window, already warming up the room.

When I reached for Granny's cookbook, which she kept on the top shelf, a tiny midnight blue jar came tumbling down. I screamed a little and caught it a mere inch before it crashed on the floor. POPPY DUST, JUST A PINCH DOES THE TRICK, the label read. "So it does," I said out loud. Last night, Granny had complained that her arm ached. She probably used a little poppy dust to help her sleep when it was particularly painful. As I returned the jar to its hideaway on the shelf, I hoped Granny would sleep at least another hour, even if it meant having to bear her terrible snoring.

I leafed through the yellowed pages of the cookbook—each recipe recorded in small, neat script—until I found BIRTHDAY CAKE. Donning Granny's favorite apron, I mixed the ingredients and poured the creamy batter into three round pans. "Now bake up nice and pretty like the ones Granny makes," I said as I slid the pans into the sweltering oven. Oh, how I wanted to be finished! But there was still frosting to be made, so with a sigh, I flipped through the cookbook again.

These recipes had been passed down from mother to daughter for three generations. My mother, Anita, would have been next in line to inherit the cookbook—if she were still alive. Thinking of her with a sudden wave of sadness, I touched the cross pendant that hung around my neck. The smooth gold felt warm against my fingertips. On its reverse side was an engraving barely visible to the naked eye. It appeared to be a sliver of a moon, with a tiny dot in its middle. The cross had been my mother's, and I wore it always. It helped me feel closer to her. Sometimes it even made me feel more like her, especially when I desperately needed to be brave.

I had no memories of my mother, and Granny told me very little about her—yet somehow I couldn't picture her baking day in and day out, like Granny, or delivering baked goods all over the village, like I do. From what I'd gleaned over the years, my mother had been a strong, wildly beautiful woman. She'd had an endless supply of the most fascinating friends and a new adventure waiting around every bend.

In other words, the very opposite of me.

I peeked in the oven and almost squealed out loud. Each layer had turned a lovely golden color with a slightly rounded top. I could have admired my sweet-smelling cake layers all morning, but I didn't want to risk burning them. After removing them from the oven, I set them on racks by the window to cool. Though it had been sunny earlier that morning, clouds had rolled in, no doubt brewing up a May shower.

Then it was back to conquering the frosting. I'd followed the recipe and beat and whipped it with all of my might for at least half an hour, so why wasn't it smooth and fluffy, like Granny's? When I fetched the cake pans from the window, I couldn't believe my eyes. It was as if someone had thrown a rock into the center of each layer. To make matters worse, when I tried to empty the first layer from its pan, it stuck. I jabbed it with a knife, but when it finally came out, it was bumpy. And the other two didn't come out any better.

"What's going on in here?" Granny asked as she

shuffled into the kitchen. With her dimples, wire-rimmed glasses, and gray hair swept into a bun, she looked like a sweet-as-molasses grandma out of a storybook. But I knew a different character, one whose whole purpose in life was to make her sixteen-year-old granddaughter as miserable as possible.

I couldn't even count to ten before the first gibe left her mouth. "You're doing it all wrong."

Biting my lip, I turned my back to her as I continued smearing globs of frosting onto the horrendously mis-shapen cake.

"Looks to me that you might have forgotten to test it," she said, pointing at the corn-husk broom that hung from a hook behind the oven.

Part of me wanted to ask for help. I loved the idea of presenting Peter with a cake so beautiful and scrumptious it would be the talk of the whole village. If anyone could accomplish making a cake so grand, it was my grand-mother. But the other part of me was much too proud to ask Granny for so much as a halfpenny, let alone admit to her that I hadn't remembered to stick a straw from the little broom into the cake to test that it was done. I couldn't bake worth a bag of beans.

Speaking of beans, "I made coffee," I said. "You should have some." Hopefully it wouldn't be long before the rich black liquid worked its magic on her mood.

"Don't you remember a blasted thing I taught you?" Granny reached for the knife, but I held it out of her reach. "Don't spread it so close to the edges."

"It's for Peter, and he won't care if it isn't perfect." I truly believed this. Peter was the one who taught me that with a bit of hard work, anything could be made beautiful. He did it every day, turning a bucketful of scrap metal into something wonderful.

"If it's in your power to make it perfect, you should never settle for anything less." Granny helped herself to a cup of coffee. "Even if it's for that blacksmith's fool of a son," she added under her breath.

"Peter's no fool," I argued, pushing up my chin. "You might grow to like him, if you'd only give him a chance." When I just started going to school, she allowed Peter to walk me home. Then, around the time I turned thirteen, she said I was safer walking through the woods alone than with the likes of Peter. I honestly didn't know what I'd said or done—or what he had said or done—to turn Granny against him. In her mind, the blacksmith's son was only after one thing, and she insisted he would not be getting that from her granddaughter—not if she and her trusty crossbow had anything to say about it. Granny tilted the cup to her lips and glugged half of it down.

"He's really nice," I tried again. "Smart, too. Maybe we can invite him over for supper someti—"

She sputtered and slammed her cup down on the counter. "If that boy sets foot in this house, I'll put an arrow right through him." As I squeezed in to fill her cup to the rim, my eyes flickered to her crossbow, which was conveniently—and ominously—propped against the back door. "And I won't aim for his heart, if you follow my drift. Maybe if I'd shot the boys who came to call on your mother . . ."

This time, I bit my lip too hard—and when I swallowed, I tasted a little blood. It was no secret Granny wished her only daughter's life had turned out differently.

I knew Granny loved me and was happy I had been born. Still, it wasn't like she'd chosen to raise me.

It didn't have to be this way forever, though. *Someday, I'm going to leave this stupid village. I'll be adventurous, like my mother was.* I'd been saving my delivery tips in a secret wooden box, waiting for the perfect time to make my grand escape. Was a happy ending too much to wish for?

As I daydreamed about all the places I'd go and people I'd meet, I absently swiped my finger around the rim of the bowl and tasted the frosting. My taste buds all but exploded, and not in a good way. *Blech.* I tried not to gag as I pondered what I'd done wrong. Had I added a tablespoon of salt when I was supposed to use a teaspoon? It looked terrible, too, I realized with mounting panic. It was the color of a witch's teeth and as lumpy as porridge. How in the world did Granny make her frosting so smooth and fluffy, and as white as freshly fallen snow?

With a heavy sigh, I plunked the knife on the countertop. I was clearly failing on my own, but asking Granny to help me make Peter's birthday cake—especially when she was already so busy and had gotten a late start on her day—would only make her more cantankerous. Whether I liked it or not, I needed Granny's permission to go to Peter's party. So I took a deep breath and relaxed my face into what I hoped was a pleasant expression. *Stay on Granny's good side, Red.*

Although, now that I thought about it, had I ever been on Granny's good side? I wasn't even sure she *had* a good side.

While Granny started whipping up breakfast, I rolled up my sleeves and scrubbed the dishes harder than necessary, trying to drown out Granny's voice as she scolded me for splattering batter on the cookbook. Like a cat about to pounce on a mouse, she paced alongside my disaster of a cake. Regrettably, the lumpy frosting did not disguise its deformities, not even a teensy bit. It actually made it look worse.

Still, did Granny think I was blind? Plain as day, it was the most pitiful excuse for a cake in the land. *So why isn't she saying anything?* My nerves were frazzled, and when I got down to my last one, I knew my plan to butter Granny up would have to wait.

"Well, Granny?" I untied the apron from my waist and slapped it onto the countertop next to the cake. "Aren't you going to tell me what a disgrace I am to the Lucas family? I'm all ears." I went back to drying dishes and continued, "Or maybe something like 'If I hadn't delivered you with my own two hands, I would've sworn you were born of trolls'?" Everyone knew that trolls were worse cooks than ogres—or even royal princesses, for that matter.

"I'm certain it will taste fine," Granny said.

The bowl I'd been drying made a terrible racket when I dropped it into the sink. "Granny, are you feeling all right? You just said something *nice*."

"It's not the first time. You just refuse to hear, or choose to forget." A shadow fell over the cottage and, seconds later, rain began to fall. "Come to the table, child. Breakfast is ready."

Before sitting, I filled Granny's cup with another serving of steaming coffee. "How many deliveries do I have today?" I asked.

"Eleven."

I nodded, relieved. Normally there were about twenty. It wouldn't take very long to bring Granny's baked goods to eleven customers, which was good news because I needed to bake a whole new cake. But Granny was quick to crush my joy. "Between stops, you'll peddle the extra goodies I baked last night. I need to find a way to bring in more money, and after thinking about it long and hard, this is the best way I see how, apart from becoming bandits."

"What do you mean?" I asked.

"They're the sorts of people who plan some kind of distraction so a carriage that is passing through must stop. Then the bandits pounce, stealing everything they can get their hands on."

I shook my head. "I know what a bandit is. But you want me to knock on random people's doors?" I couldn't think of anything more humiliating than begging strangers to buy a crumpet. Clutching my fork tightly, I stuffed a large piece of flapjack into my mouth. "If I'm always making deliveries and having to sell goods door-to-door," I continued between chews, "when will I find time to study my lessons, or go to the swimming hole, or spend time with my friends?" As I spluttered the bit about friends, a lump of chewed-up flapjack lodged in my throat.

My coughing caught Granny's attention, and she raised her eyebrows in alarm. "Gracious, child!" She flung her fork across the floor and sprung up like a snake had bitten her bottom. Her chair toppled over as she chopped my back with the side of her hand, one strike for each word: "There's. A. Reason. You're. Not. Supposed. To. Talk. With. Your. Mouth. Full!"

"I'm *fine*, Granny," I said as best I could with a madwoman beating my back. "Stop it! I just need a swig of milk, that's all."

When I finally convinced her I wasn't choking to death, she righted her chair and sat down quietly, strands of hair falling loose from her bun. From her flashing green eyes, I could tell she remained on high alert. She'd already lost her only daughter, and I had a feeling that to keep me safe from harm, she'd fight anyone—or anything—to the death. Even inanimate objects like flapjacks.

Granny wasted little time before looping back to

the topic of my dreaded new duty. Of all the grandmas in the world, I was stuck with one whose memory was as sharp as a dragon's claw. "Yes, you'll go door-to-door hawking baked goods. Might not sound appealing, but you'll live."

Before I could hold my tongue, I muttered, "Ugh. Sounds even more miserable than being cooped up in the cottage with you."

"No use complaining," Granny said. "It must be done."

"But, why? I know I complained that all the other girls had new springtime frocks and boots, but honestly, I'll get by just fine with what I have."

Granny rolled the hem of her apron with her calloused fingers. Three flapjacks were stacked on her tin plate, drizzled with maple syrup and dolloped with creamy butter. She hadn't taken a bite, not even a nibble—which was quite a feat, considering that as far as I was concerned, her flapjacks were the fluffiest in the land.

I listened to myself chewing, and it made me ponder if people chitchatted at meals so they didn't have to hear each other sipping, slurping, and smacking. "Are you going to eat those?" I asked when the silence grew uncomfortable. "Because if not, I'll be happy to finish them up for you."

Without a word, she slid her plate across the table. I hacked off a big bite with my fork. While I chewed, Granny went back to picking at the fabric of her apron. Oh, no. Granny never surrendered her flapjacks. *What have I said to upset her this much?* "All right, all right. I'll try my best to get some new regulars today," I said once I'd swallowed. "Don't worry, Granny. Your treats sell themselves."

While I cleared the table, Granny started wrapping the baked goods for delivery. If I could sell everything in my basket, maybe it would please her so much she might even consider letting me go to Peter's party. What good was having any hope at all if I didn't reach for the moon?

Two

Basket in hand and riding hood draped over my head and shoulders, I took off for the village. The rain had tapered down to a mere mist. I loved the sweet, earthy smell of the forest after a good rain shower, and I took a moment to fill my lungs with the dewy air.

I walked backwards, watching our cottage steadily shrink into the distance. My grandmother's six brothers had built the house long ago, back when they were young men—before the wolf had attacked them and slashed their throats as she'd watched helplessly from the roof.

I hoped beyond hope that I'd never, ever witness anything as frightful as a bloodthirsty monster killing people I loved. Tears pricked my eyes as I thought about that tragic night, so I quickly pushed the thought aside; instead I pictured the cottage at its finest, before the log walls needed oiling and the thatched, steeply sloped roof needed patching. Before the oak tree had grown tall and strong enough to support the rope swing I'd spent countless hours on.

I imagined my mother had grown up swinging on that very rope, too. There was a time when the window boxes burst with flowers of every shape and color—but it had been years since Granny had planted new ones, or trimmed back the ferns that covered the stone path leading to the front door, or the one out back that meandered to the stream. It had been years since the village children gathered by the fireplace while Granny read storybooks and baked more shortbread cookies than our little bellies could hold. These memories consumed me as I turned my back on the cottage and plodded down the muddy road into the village.

Perhaps the door-to-door selling wouldn't be so bad after all. I took a deep breath and rapped on the door of a rickety little house of the far west side of town. While I waited, my heartbeat hastened. I ran my fingertips along the gold cross that dangled from my neck.

A burly, shirtless man stood in the doorway, looking as if he'd been sleeping, and smelling as if he hadn't bathed since last Wolfstime.

"Whatdayawant, girl?" he slurred.

"Have you ever heard of Granny's Baked Goods?" I asked, hoping to sound much more enthusiastic than I felt. I didn't even give him a chance to respond. "Well, if you haven't, you've been missing out."

"What? What're you yakking about, girl?"

I tittered nervously. "Allow me to introduce myself. I'm Red." I held my hand out and he shook it limply in his sweaty grasp. "I've come by your lovely home to see if you'd like any of my grandmother's delicious baked goods. They're all made fresh, using only the finest ingredients."

"Red? What kind of name is that?"

"It's a nickname."

"But you're not a redhead."

"I know. They call me 'Red' because . . . Never mind. Look, I have some delicious croissants here—" I waved my hand over the basket like I'd seen the street magicians do at market.

The man pulled a face. All right, so croissants weren't his favorite. "—as well as a variety of cookies and muffins," I continued brightly. "You look like a muffin man to me."

"Well, I might . . ."

"Fantastic! For today's special bargain price, you can have your choice of bran or blueber—"

"How 'bout I try one first, to make sure it's edible and all?"

I sighed. "I'm afraid I don't have enough for sampling. However, I know you'll love Granny's muffins. My grandmother has never, ever baked anything less than perfection. It's her special talent."

He raised an enormous eyebrow. I could tell he was tempted, and I held my breath in hopeful anticipation . . .

"No." He started to close the door, but I held it ajar with my foot.

"No?"

"No."

"All right, then," I said, my heart sinking. "Would you like me to come back tomorrow?"

"No."

I winced as the door slammed shut in my face. "How about next week?" I said to no one but a little brown spider crawling on the armrest of the rocking chair.

Two hours later, I'd made a total of ten regular deliveries, and though I'd knocked on countless doors hoping to sell Granny's extras, I had nothing to show for it. Discouraged and more than a little annoyed at having wasted so much time, I climbed the steps leading to Seamstress Evans's house, the eleventh and final delivery of the day.

She had ordered a half-dozen crumpets and an apple pie for her family, and as payment she handed me a couple of coins, a spool of yellow thread, and four wooden buttons. "I wish it were more, Red, but times are tough," she apologized. "With taxes due, it's all I can spare. But I'll pay you properly next time, I promise."

Once the door closed, I reached in my pouch to count up the tips that the customers had given me: barely enough to make up for what the seamstress lacked, plus two unsold cookies and four muffins. The day's sales could have gone better—much better, really. My heart felt heavy as I straightened my hood, picked up my basket, and marched back toward home.

One of Seamstress Evans's little boys, a toddler with muddy knees and a pirate hat, jumped out from behind a bush and shouted, "Argh! Hand over your booty an' no one gets hurt!"

"Oh, *my*. If you're looking for treasure, Cap'n, this is your lucky day," I said. "Now, close your eyes . . ." I bundled the cookies and muffins in a handkerchief and set them under an apple tree in his plain sight, because of course he was peeking in between his fingers the whole time. He dutifully waited a few seconds and then made a run for the treasure. Suddenly, and out of nowhere, four other children tackled him to the ground, poking him with wooden swords.

"You'd better share it with your mateys, Cap'n," I called over my shoulder, laughing. Playing with the Evans children made me long for little brothers and sisters of my own. But I knew that a big family was a foolish thing to wish for, since my parents were long gone. Some girls in the village, like my former schoolmate Priscilla, had already started their own families. I wanted to have my own children, too. But I couldn't imagine that it would be any time soon. I wanted to leave this village and have my fair share of adventures first.

Drops of rain glistened from the leaves, and the springtime early-evening sun beamed through the trees. Twigs and pinecones crunched under my boots, and a pair of yellow butterflies flitted just above my head. When I neared the swimming hole, I heard splashing followed by Peter's husky voice. *"Hallo, Red!"*

I pulled back a tree branch to clear my view. From the deepest point of the pond, he waved at me and grinned. "Come on in; the water's fine," he called.

The temptation was strong, but I knew I shouldn't.

"Oh, Peter. I wish I could, but I need to get home to Granny," I said ruefully.

Peter's smile faltered. We'd been friends forever—in fact, he was probably my only true friend. He climbed out of the pond and onto a boulder, where he shook the water out of his mop of dark hair. His bare chest squeezed in and out as he caught his breath.

He'd had sun-kissed skin and kind brown eyes for as long as I remembered, but when exactly had he shot up taller than me? And when had that shadow of whiskers on his jawline appeared? I couldn't help noticing how handsome, how *grown-up*, my friend Peter had become.

Before he could see that I was blushing, I tore my gaze away from him and stared instead at my shoes. Sunbeams pierced through the branches above, lighting up my dusty, shabby boots until they practically glowed. I bit my lower lip as the sun's warmth rained down on me.

A quick dip wouldn't hurt anything, would it?

April, ten years ago

As Peter and I walked home from school together, he told me a story. "This morning, Papa went into his shop to start working. He began doing his prep work, and everything seemed normal enough. But then, from the darkest corner of the forge, he heard a strange noise—a scuffling sound, and then a broom toppled right over! Papa said, 'Who's there?' No one answered. And then the scuffling noise happened again, even louder!"

"What then?" I asked, completely mesmerized. Goose bumps dotted my arms as if I were right there. It helped that I'd been in his father's workshop before, and with all the weapon-like tools, banging and crashing noises, and sparking, blazing fires, my imagination ran wild. The first time I'd been there, I'd felt like I was trapped in a deep, dark dungeon by a ferocious fire-breathing dragon. The memory took hold of me, and I hoped against hope that Peter's father was able to vanquish whatever evil force had come into his shop to do him in. "Come on, Peter, don't keep me waiting. Tell me what happened next!"

"Papa picked up an anvil." Peter smiled. I liked it

when he grinned like that. It made me want to walk closer to him, to count how many teeth he'd lost already. "He held it as tight as he could," he continued, "and the closer he got to the noise, the louder it sounded."

"What then? Come *on*, Peter. Tell me!" I could hardly stand the suspense.

"Papa said, 'Whoever you are, come out this instant.'"

"And did they come out? Who was it?"

"Oh, yes, it came out all right. It was a . . . skunk."

I laughed. "A skunk? Really?"

"Cross my heart. And it sprayed the dickens out of him!"

I doubled over with laughter. "Oh, that is so funny! Oops, I mean, *horrible*. Your poor father!"

"You can say that again. Mama didn't let him come to breakfast, and she'd made his favorite: flapjacks."

I rubbed my belly. "My favorite, too. Now I *really* feel sorry for him."

"Well, the story does have a happy ending. I got to eat every last bit of Papa's breakfast."

I laughed some more, and my belly ached with happiness until we got to the cottage. The front door swung open as if Granny had been peeking out the window, waiting like a hunter waits for a stag. "Who's this?" she asked, eyeing my friend.

"This is Peter. He walked me home from school." I almost told her about how we'd discovered our footsteps were almost exactly the same length, so neither of us ever had to jog to keep up with the other. I had a feeling she wouldn't care anything about that, though.

Peter offered his hand for a shake, and when she took it, she rolled it over. "Your fingernails are black."

"His papa is the blacksmith," I said proudly. "Peter gets to be his apprentice someday." I could only dream what it was like to have a father. Or a mother. Or an exciting trade to look forward to learning and taking over once I grew up.

Peter explained politely, "I really do wash my hands, ma'am. Fact is, most of it's just too stubborn to get off, no matter how hard I scrub at it."

Granny clicked her tongue. "Your pants are tattered, as well."

Peter looked down at his trousers like he'd never noticed them before. "I'll ask my mama to mend them soon as I get home," he promised.

"That's a grand idea. Now, Peter, why did you walk my granddaughter home?"

"Seemed like the thing to do." He shrugged. "Might like to do it again tomorrow. If it's all right with you, ma'am."

I puffed up my chest, hoping she'd say yes. Walking home with somebody was a lot more fun than being all alone. And Peter—with his gappy grin and entertaining stories—was especially fun.

Granny bent down and stared him right in his eyes.

He blinked; however, he never flinched or backed away.

I was sure she was going to say no. She surprised me. "I suppose that will be all right. But I'll be watching you."

"All right, Peter. Just one jump," I agreed now, climbing the highest rock.

His eyes grew half a size. "From way up there?"

"Where else?" After setting down my basket and shedding my dress, boots, and stockings, I reached up into the sky and took a deep breath.

"It's just that I've never seen a girl do it," he said.

I put my hands on my hips. "I've seen you jump a hundred times. So it must be as easy as cake." Then again, after baking Peter's cake that morning, I should definitely have stopped using that particular expression. It might have been easy for some people, like Granny, but not for me.

My remark got a scoff out of Peter, which made me smile. Until I glanced down. I hadn't realized it was remotely this high. The whole forest whirled and churned before my eyes. I took several steps back, steadying myself on the rock behind me.

"You can come back down any time now, Red. I know you want to," Peter said, sounding frustratingly amused.

"Oh, don't you worry, Peter. I'm going to jump. I'm

just enjoying the scenery from up here." *And trying not to throw up.* With my big toe, I scooted a pile of pebbles off the edge. It seemed to take five full minutes for them to pelt the water below, finally causing a starburst of ripples.

"The longer you put it off, the scarier it is," Peter said.

Out of habit, I reached for the gold cross pendant. A feeling that my mother had stood on this very rock overwhelmed me. It was like a memory, if that were even possible—of her jumping off from this very point and landing in the water below, a breathtaking combination of grace and bravery.

"It's all right, Red. Your secret is safe with me."

"What secret?" I looked up guiltily. Did he somehow know that I'd been spending so much time trying to imagine my mother?

"That you're . . ." He flapped his arms at his sides and clucked.

I sighed in relief and put my hands on my hips. "I am not chicken!"

"Then prove it." Peter counted down, "Three . . .

two . . . *one*," and I shut my eyes, held my nose, and leapt. The wind ripped through my hair as I fell, and I swore I heard a voice say, *Breathe.* I plunged deep into the shockingly cool water. It took me a few seconds to get my bearings. I struggled to swim with the weight and bulk of my petticoats. When I finally surfaced, I rolled onto my back and filled my lungs with the springtime air. I felt so wonderful, so free; I couldn't help laughing out loud. When I turned to look for Peter on the bank, he was gone. *Where is he?* Had he left before I'd jumped? After all of that, had he missed it?

"Look out belooooow!" Peter hollered down from where I'd leapt. After flipping around twice, he tucked his body into a ball and drenched me with a tidal wave of a splash. Not a minute later, he was treading water next to me, chuckling as if the whole thing had been completely effortless for him.

After paddling to the edge of the water, I lugged myself up onto the bank, where I sat watching Peter swim hither and yon.

It was hard to fathom a time when Peter couldn't swim, but he used to be afraid. When he was seven, he told the other boys his mama didn't want him getting water in his ears and other such nonsense. I said, "You know, Peter, you can't learn to swim if you never jump in the water." Finally, he took a big, deep breath and leapt right in. He flailed his arms and swallowed a bunch of water, but the more he paddled about, the more at home he felt in the water. In all the times I'd spent with him there at the pond, he'd become a strong swimmer. Actually, he'd become strong, period.

When Peter decided to join me on the shore, he sprawled out, resting his head in his hands. His dark hair was slicked back, making him look so different, almost royal. We laid beside each other on the soft ground, soaking in the warm sunlight. Every so often, I turned my head to gaze at him, but never long enough for him to notice.

A few minutes later, Peter sat up and stretched. He stared beyond the pond into the trees. "There's barely a tree in this entire forest that doesn't have a wanted poster stuck on it," he said, his eyes narrowing. "It's like every man and his dog is a crook these days. Women and children, too. Can you believe it? I really hate thieves. They're nothing but a bunch of lowlifes without a lick of honor."

"I can't imagine ever getting desperate enough to steal," I said. Then, suddenly horrified, I turned to him and added, "I didn't mean any offense by that, Peter. You know, your uncle . . ."

When Peter had been a little boy, his favorite uncle had been an expert pickpocket. His uncle taught Peter how to do it, and sometimes, for fun, Peter would swipe something out of his parents' or brothers'—or even my— pockets. Of course, he'd always give back whatever he'd taken; and I, for one, could never figure out how or when he'd stolen from me.

As for his uncle, in time, he sought greater challenges, and he began robbing carriages deep in the woods. I'd never forget the day Peter and I saw the poster with a sketch of his very own uncle, a wanted bandit. With dis- appointment etched on his face, Peter threw rocks into the pond until his arms ached. Peter never saw or heard from his favorite uncle again. We never saw another of his wanted posters, either. We could only guess that he'd been captured and turned in for the ransom, and he was fated to spend the rest of his days locked up in the royal castle's dungeon.

"He got what was coming to him," Peter said, shaking his head. And just like that, his almost-dry hair relaxed into its typical tousles.

I looked up at the trees, clouds, and sky, and while my mind wandered, I felt his warm gaze on my face. *What does Peter see in me?* I wondered. In his eyes, was I still that giggly six-year-old girl?

"You look . . ." he started, and then swallowed loudly.

I smiled as I waited for him to say that I looked beautiful or refreshed, or—though it would've been a bit of a mouthful—like the girl he was destined to have the first dance with at the Forget-Me-Not ball.

The whole notion of a ball was rather silly. It wasn't like we had lavish clothes or food, let alone a ballroom. Still, it was an age-old tradition for our village. Named after the forget-me-not flowers that grew on the edges of the forest, it was supposed to help everybody remember their childhoods as they moved on into their adult lives.

Honestly, I didn't really care about going to the ball, and last summer, Peter and I had agreed to spend the evening at our swimming hole instead. But sometimes, when I least expected it, a daydream about dancing with Peter at the Forget-Me-Not ball popped into my head.

"You look like a drowned rat sitting on a giant mushroom," Peter said.

It took a moment for his words to sink in. Though it wasn't the compliment I'd hoped for, his description was probably spot-on. "Really, Peter!" I crossed my arms over my chest. "You sure know how to make a girl feel special."

Tugging the edge of my billowing white petticoat, Peter pulled me close. The spark in his eyes softened. "The cutest drowned rat on a giant mushroom that I've ever seen."

I laughed, despite myself. "Why, thank you. I think."

Three

"Where've you been?" Granny demanded when I walked through the door, and the smile on my face instantly vanished. She set down her knitting and said, "Gracious, child. You're a soggy mess."

"Making all the deliveries and peddling your goods door-to-door made me hot and tired, so I took a quick dip in the swimming hole." I plucked a twig out of my hair as I made my way to the kitchen and set the basket on the countertop.

"You should've been born with gills," she said. "When you were three, you jumped into the swimming hole without a second thought. It scared me to death, so I went in after you. Didn't even think to take off my boots, let alone my glasses."

"I know, Granny. You've told me that story a hundred times. Maybe a thousand. Here you go." I dropped the tips I'd received into her palm.

"What's this for?"

"The extra cookies and muffins," I said, a little white lie.

She stared at the money. "So no one bought the pies?"

"Not today. Maybe tomorrow." I smiled encouragingly and took a breath, trying to broach the subject of Peter's birthday party. I had the sinking sensation that Granny wouldn't allow me to go out tonight. First off, it was a party for Peter—and it was no secret she didn't trust him as far as she could throw him. And most importantly, it was nearing Wolfstime.

Even though tonight's moon wouldn't be completely full, Granny's paranoia grew with each successive Wolfstime. "The pack is growing larger," she'd said at the last town meeting. "The more wolves roaming the forest, the more they'll need to eat. The more they'll hunt. Sometime in the near future, the full moon will mean nothing. They'll hunt every night, even the darkest. Mark my words. . . ."

Granny had spoken with great conviction that evening, and my cheeks had flared when the villagers poked one another and sniggered behind her back. I'd been ashamed, and instead of standing beside her, I'd slipped out to the fountain and lost myself in daydreams of the places I'd someday travel to.

Peter had invited me to his party three days ago. Since then, it had been the talk of the school yard. We were like a bunch of squirrels, eager to get out after a particularly long winter. I'd gone along with the crowd, saying things such as, "Of course I'll be there. I wouldn't dream of missing it."

Violet had singled me out. "Don't be ridiculous, Red. Your grandmother will *never* give you permission."

Everybody had poked one another and laughed behind my back, making me feel like Granny must have felt at the last town meeting. Violet had that kind of effect on people. She was likely the prettiest girl in the whole village, and she was smart, as well. People listened to her, followed her, and fawned over her. If anything important or exciting was happening, she was always in the center of it. She was never invisible.

I'd straightened my shoulders. "Did you not hear me, Violet? I *said* I'll be there, and I will."

Since then, I'd been grasping at the slightest sliver of hope that something would come over my grand-mother and she'd grant me permission. I'd heard of fairy godmothers appearing out of thin air and making girls' dreams come true. Perhaps this was my night! In one final act of desperation, I closed my eyes and took a deep breath . . .

Yet nothing happened.

Of course it didn't. I just needed to admit to myself that Violet was right. No matter how nicely I asked, or how winsome a case I presented, Granny wasn't going to let me out tonight. I was stuck at home. I might as well have been locked up with Peter's uncle in the royal castle's dungeon.

"I made too much frosting today," Granny said out of the blue. She pointed at a bowl by the sink, covered with a checkered cloth. "And I've been baking so much more than usual; I've plumb run out of storage." She shook her head sadly while I peeked under the napkin at the bowl full of snow-white fluffiness.

"It's perfect."

Granny harrumphed. "It is what it is. Anyhow, if you could just do something with it. Toss it out—or better yet, feed it to Farmer Thompson's pigs."

"Yes, Granny." As I scooped a finger full into my mouth and its delicious sweetness exploded on my tongue, I tried not to grin. I knew what my grandmother was up to, and I was beyond grateful. She turned on her heel and left me alone with Peter's birthday cake. I hummed as I scraped off the old lumpy stuff and replaced it with her delicious frosting, mindful not to get it too close to the edges in between the layers, like she'd taught me. Finally, I stepped back and admired the result. *Peter will love it!* I couldn't wait to give it to him later that night.

The cake was a sign.

When I passed through the living room, where Granny had taken up her knitting again, I gave myself one last chance. "Granny?" I started.

"Hmmm?"

I couldn't do it. I could not ask her permission and risk her saying no and putting me on stricter-than-normal lockdown. The only way I could go to Peter's bonfire—the only way I could spend more time with Peter on his birthday and give him the cake *and* prove Violet wrong—was to sneak out tonight. "I'm going to go clean myself up now."

"All right, but don't dillydally. We have to prepare the house."

"I know, I know." I would've liked soaking in the tub, but I knew Granny was waiting. She'd never been the patient sort. So I simply changed into fresh clothes, taking extra care in brushing out my hair. Since I'd looked like a drowned rat after we'd gone swimming earlier that day, I wanted Peter to see me at my best at his party. Sometimes, while the boys and I amused ourselves with archery or swimming, they mentioned that other girls at the school—in particular Violet, Florence, and Beatrice—were beautiful and smelled of honeysuckle. I wondered if Peter ever said that I was fair or smelled of something sweet.

I leaned closer to my reflection. Something didn't seem right. Something was missing. Gasping, I slid my fingers along my collarbone, in case it really was there and the mirror was deceiving me. No such fortune.

"Oh, no!" I exclaimed. I dropped to my knees, searching the floor and my discarded clothes for my mother's golden cross necklace.

"What's taking you so long, child?" Granny called from the living room.

I tried to calm myself, breathing slowly in and out, like the voice in my Wolfstime dreams told me to do.

The last memory I had of my treasured heirloom was right before I jumped into the pond that afternoon with Peter. It must have fallen off! It could be in the water or among the rocks or along the bank—or anywhere at all I'd wandered since then. Was I a fool to believe I'd ever see it again, when it was like a needle in a haystack? Maybe if I could sneak out of the house early enough, I could take a quick detour to the swimming hole on my way to the bonfire, before darkness set in. Otherwise, I'd have to wait until morning to even begin looking for the lost necklace.

"Coming, Granny." With a crushed heart, I hurried to my bedroom window. A scrawny gray squirrel squatted on a branch just outside. "Well, hello there," I greeted him. He sniffed the air and then scurried down the tree and off into the rosebushes. "You don't have to be rude," I admonished him before pulling the shutters closed.

After Granny drifted to sleep that night—with the help of some of the poppy dust I'd found in the kitchen sprinkled into her cider—I planned to climb out of my window and go to Peter's party. My red cloak would protect me if a wolf were on the prowl. I took my cloak off the bedpost and draped it around my body, the embrace of the magical garment making me feel instantly and completely safe.

November, three and a half years ago

"Get in here, young lady! Now." I wasn't sure how many times she'd yelled for me because I'd been swinging, leaning back as far as possible without toppling over, watching for a shooting star. I knew I'd get a wish when I blew out my birthday candles, but I had a really important one to make this year, and wishing on two things was always better than just one. At least that's what I figured. If I could've found a genie, I would've wished all three of those wishes as well.

"Just another minute, Granny," I pleaded. "I promise I'll come in real soon. I'm just not quite finished out here, that's all." *Come on, shooting star, where are you? Where, oh where, are you?*

"Oh, you're finished, young lady." Granny grabbed me by the shoulder and marched me through the back door, all the while mumbling about how any girl in her right mind could spend so many hours on an old rope swing was beyond her. "Now, sit here. I'll be right back. I said, *sit*." I flopped onto the sofa, crossing my arms over my chest.

She disappeared into the kitchen, snuffing out the candles on the mantel and table as she went. It seemed to be taking her an awfully long time. The wind howled outside the windows, and tree branches clawed against the roof. It felt like something scary was trying to come inside. "Granny?" I called, my voice quivering in the shadows.

Finally, she came back, her face aglow with the thirteen candles that lit up my birthday cake. I smiled, feeling silly for having let fright get the best of me.

"Make a wish, child," Granny said. The cake was as

white as snow, so perfect it hardly seemed real. I doubted that even a princess would have a birthday cake as pretty as mine.

I closed my eyes and took a deep breath—probably the deepest one I'd ever taken. Then I peeked out of one eye, just to make sure the flames were still right in front of my lips.

I wish I could leave this village to find my happy ending!

I blasted the candles with all the air in my lungs, and they *poofed* out, one by one. Pleased, I clapped my hands together. I could almost feel the wish working, and part of me wanted to run to my room and count the coins I'd been collecting in my secret box—my "Adventure Fund."

"Good work. Now for your present," Granny said. She relit the candles around us and then handed me a big box, perfectly square, wrapped in the most elegant gold paper and a silky red ribbon. I gasped. "It's beautiful."

"Well, it's definitely something," Granny agreed. "You're thirteen now. You're practically a woman. Go on, open it already."

At first, I took my time, not wanting to rip the paper. But that was taking too long, and I was dying to see what wonderful gift Granny had gotten for me. I wasn't sure what it was, even as I peered into the open box.

All I could see was red.

I pulled my gift out and held it at arm's length. The hooded cloak was made of rich red fabric, a lovely brocade on the outside, and lined in lush velvet. I stood and tried it on, loving how the hood draped over my braids and the cape flowed to the ground so regally. I couldn't wait to wear it to school; I knew I'd be the envy of all the other girls.

"Do you like it?" Granny asked.

I twirled, admiring how it floated in the air and then, as soon as I stopped, landed so gently around my ankles. It felt like wings and butterfly kisses rolled into one. "Oh, Granny. It's wonderful!"

She nodded. "It's no ordinary hood. Now, sit back down and I'll tell you all about it." Once I stopped twirling and sat beside her, she continued. "First off, the color red repels wolves. Plus, I had a wizard place a magic spell on it. See here?"

Pinned to the bottom of the cloak was a square of parchment, and upon it was written in midnight blue ink:

WEAR THIS GARMENT, FEAR NOT THE WOLF.

"The wizard wrote this?" I asked.

"Of course."

"But I thought you said to stay away from magic. That even when it's used for good, it can change to something very bad."

She nodded. "It's true, but in this case, I did what I had to do to keep you safe. This magic cloak will protect you from the wolves, my dear. You must wear it every Wolfstime," Granny said. "Promise me."

I drew the cloak tightly around my body, trembling at the very thought of the wolves. I never knew my grandfather or my great-uncles. I had no memories of my mother or my father. One way or another, the wolves were the reason they were dead.

I held the gold cross that had been my mother's between my fingers. "I promise."

I shivered with the knowledge that soon the forest would be on the cusp of Wolfstime. My fingers grazed my neck, but the golden cross wasn't there to soothe me this time. I pulled my cloak taut around my shoulders as I joined Granny in the living room.

"Who were you talking to?" Granny asked. Though her bones creaked and her skin was wrinkled, it never ceased to amaze me how well her ears worked.

"Just a squirrel. A very ornery squirrel."

"*Humph.* And people say *I'm* crazy," Granny muttered, shaking her head. I opened my mouth to say that no one thought she was crazy—which was, of course, a lie—but she cut me off. "No time for chin-wag. We've work to do." The staid look she shot me warned me not to argue.

I helped her lift the planks and wedge them securely

against the front and back doors. Next I hurried around the cottage securing shutters and locking windows while she pulled the iron portcullis down over the fireplace. Rubbing her right arm, she leaned against the wall to catch her breath. I hated seeing her in such pain and so very exhausted. *It will be good for her to get a good night's sleep tonight.*

"Sit down, Granny," I said, guiding her to a chair. "I'll get us both a nice cup of cider."

"Yes, yes. That sounds nice."

When I returned from the kitchen, Granny was fixated on the door. "The hunters are going out tonight, you know. They're nothing but stupid, idiotic fools! Thinking they can kill the wolves. Someone's going to die one of these nights, I feel it in my bones," she said, rubbing her right arm.

Last full moon, the village was misfortunate enough to lose two lambs and five chickens to the wolves. But Granny remembered a time long, long ago, when people strolled through the village, caught up in games or music or love, and didn't heed the warnings. They didn't pay attention, they were risky, they indulged in drink—and those gaffes proved fatal. The morning after, when the sun shone the light of truth, their bloody, ripped-apart, feasted-upon remains were strewn up and down the cobblestone streets of the village. For all to see, for all to fear.

Some people claimed that it had never really happened; that the tale had been passed down through the ages to frighten children into staying indoors at night. Much like stories of evil giants who used children's bones to pick food out of their teeth, or witches who fed boys and girls delectable sweets to fatten them up before feasting on their tender flesh. Still, Granny told that story with such passion; my heart filled with fear.

"We will be safe here," Granny said. As she lowered herself onto the comfy old sofa, her hand gestured broadly around us—at the cluttered bookshelf and sooty stone fireplace, the rag rug she'd woven herself, the sun-faded gingham curtains, the lopsided beeswax candles we lit every evening—and finally, she patted the space beside her on the sofa I'd never fully seen, since it had been covered in a worn calico quilt for as long as I could remember. It was the same sofa that my mother must have sat upon every day when she was alive. Maybe my father had sat on it when he'd asked Granny for her blessing to marry my mother. I placed the mugs of cider on the table, careful to set the one with the pinch of poppy dust closest to her.

"We can only hope the wolves will find their fill of livestock and chickens and leave the hunters be." She shook her head, and a section of her hair fell loose, flopping down well past her shoulders. I tucked it back into her bun for her, like I used to do when I was younger. Now the gesture seemed to make Granny uneasy. The expression on her face, like she wanted to tell me something important yet couldn't quite talk herself into it, reminded me of all the times I'd begged her to tell me how my mother and father had died.

The stories that the villagers told never seemed to

add up. Some claimed they'd been killed by wolves. Others said that my parents just woke one morning and decided to pack up and move to another village, far, far away. But why would they have left their baby daughter behind? I'd been much too young to have brewed up any real trouble yet. If I had a daughter, even if she were a rascal, I'd never, ever run away without her. I refused to believe it could be true about my own mother and father.

When I was ten, Granny finally gave in to my relentless questioning and told me what had really happened. Hunters mistook my parents for wolves deep in the forest and killed them. I immediately hated the hunters and demanded to know their names so I could get revenge as soon as I was old enough. Granny made me calm down, insisting that it wasn't the hunters' fault; they were only trying to protect the village.

The night before they died had been a particularly gruesome one in which a wolf had killed a shepherd boy, so the hunters were riled up. My parents should not have been running through the village—let alone the forest—during Wolfstime. It was reckless of them, Granny told me. Between tears, I said I bet they'd died holding hands, shot by a single arrow through both of their hearts. Granny nodded and said she was sure that was how it happened.

"Hand me my crossbow," Granny said now. I did as I was told, and then we sipped our ciders in silence—a quietness that only made the *ticktocks* of the grandfather clock seem lethargic and the wind outside sound angrier. Right before nodding off, she murmured, "Don't you worry, child. We will be safe. We will be safe . . . here."

Granny had barricaded the front door to keep unwelcome visitors out—and also to keep me trapped inside. Not tonight, though. I'd only stay at Peter's bonfire long enough to give him the cake and wish him a happy birthday, and then I'd hurry home. With any luck, Granny would never know I'd gone.

I spread a wool blanket over her and slunk into the kitchen. While carefully packing the cake in my basket, a thought occurred to me: how would I explain the missing cake to Granny? If she slept past the rooster's crow tomorrow morning—which was entirely possible with the poppy dust—I could tell her I changed my mind about giving it to Peter and fed it to Farmer Thompson's pigs. It wasn't the best plan, but it was the only one I had, so I'd have to go with it.

After taking my bow and quiver off the bureau in my bedroom—accounting for the silver-tipped arrow Peter had made me—I paused to listen. Sure enough, Granny's snores rumbled steadily through the cottage. Holding my breath, I opened the shutters and balanced my basket on the rosebushes below my window while I slipped outside. As soon as my boots hit the dirt, the squirrel hissed and twitched his whiskers. Then he scampered away and disappeared into the hedge, like before.

The wind blew, and the leaves rustled and waved, reminding me of the ripples in the swimming hole when I'd kicked the gravel from the jumping rock. If I could have gone back in time, I never would have leapt. It had given me a wonderful rush, but it hadn't been worth

losing my golden cross. As the sun dipped into the west-
ernmost sky, I knew I'd have to wait until the morning
to search for it.

I trudged through the forest, wondering if my mother
had ever snuck out of the cottage while Granny slept. I
suspected she had. How else would she have been able
to make, and keep, the most fascinating of friends? How
else would she have been able to seek adventure around
every bend? And now I was off on my own adventure; it
felt good to be so bold, so free.

Four

January, five years ago

The blizzard finally tapered off, and Granny told me to bundle up; we were going out. I fetched the matching pink scarf and mittens she'd knitted me for Christmas and the bow and arrows I never left home without. Although my boots sank into the fluffy white powder with each step, I quickly caught up with her. Robins glided over our heads, and squirrels shuttled acorns from tree to tree.

I desperately wanted to stop and build a snowman, but Granny held up a slip of paper and said, "Frolicking in the snow is not on the list." I bit back my disappointment and plodded along, mesmerized by the bluebird sky and the way the snow sparkled like diamonds. "First on the list: the blacksmith's shop to get a dozen arrowheads," Granny said, and I was suddenly glad to be included in this errand. Peter would probably be busy, but perhaps he could take a brief break.

While Granny bartered with Peter's father, I waited by a table on the front porch of their house. The table had been cleared of snow, and a small potted spruce served as a centerpiece. I wondered if they took their meals outside, even in the wintertime. Peter's folks had four boys, yet their cottage was smaller than ours. I figured that made it easier to keep tidy and warm. I liked that it had so many windows, and that I could see clear to the windmill from their porch.

Out of nowhere, something pelted me in the arm. Instinctively, I stood and reached for my bow. But then I relaxed. It was only a snowball. Brushing off the powder, I called out, "Show yourself! Or are you too chicken?"

There was a sharp whistle, followed by the clomping

of boots. Pausing only long enough to scoop a fistful of snow, I took off after whoever it was, heading for the blacksmith's shop behind the cottage. Peter was in the back of the room, working.

"I'll admit you're fast, but did you really think you'd get away from me, Peter?" I pitched my snowball at him, hitting him square in the nose.

My perfect aim must have left him speechless. He just stared at me, the clump of snow sliding down his face and onto his big black apron, his hammer frozen mid-strike over the anvil. *"Hallo,"* he said, finally. "Nice to see you."

Giggles erupted from behind the bales of hay. A moment later, a pair of bundled-up little boys spilled out of the workshop and into the snowy yard. I bit my lip and gave my classmate an awkward shrug. "Um, sorry about that. I thought you threw a snowball at me," I explained, feeling stupid.

He laughed and wiped the melting snow off his chin. "I'll forgive you. But only if you do something for me."

I arched my right eyebrow, not too keen about owing him anything.

"Bring me that pail full of scrap metal."

I did as he asked, grateful that his favor was so simple. Heavy, but simple. "What are you making?" I asked.

"I'm finished helping Papa with his orders for the week. Now I get to make something for myself. Or, maybe, for someone else. And I know just the thing." He quirked his mouth into a near-smile, and I felt myself grinning back.

I hopped onto a bale of hay and watched Peter work. In the furnace, he heated up the metal to a bright yellow-orange. Next he set it on an anvil and beat it repeatedly with a hammer, making sparks fly. For a twig of a boy, he could sure pound! He whistled while he worked. I didn't recognize the tune, but it was a happy one. "You know the best thing about being a blacksmith?" he asked.

"Getting to play with fire?" I guessed.

"Ah, yes. That is a good one. But my favorite thing is seeing potential in something that most people wouldn't.

Like these scraps. Just a heap of old junk in most people's eyes. With a little smithy magic, it can become something beautiful."

"So, what is it?" I asked, unable to hide my curiosity any longer. "What are you making?"

"What's that Miss Landon is always saying?" he prompted.

"Who put this frog in my desk?" I said, doing my best impression of our crotchety teacher.

Peter chuckled. "Well, she has been saying that quite a bit, ever since my little brothers started school. But the correct answer is, 'patience is a virtue.'" Once the metal cooled to a dark gray hue, he grabbed a file off the wall and ran it across his creation. Then he turned his back to me and said, "Sorry, but you can't watch this part. It's a family secret. The smithy magic at work."

If Granny had been there, she'd have said that was a load of poppycock. However, I didn't want to sound like a cantankerous old woman, so I just crossed my arms over my chest and tried to act aloof. "Fine, but, to be perfectly honest, I'm getting rather bored waiting around. Besides, my grandmother is probably looking for me." I knew that if that were true, she would've found me by then. When it came to tracking me down, Granny had an uncanny knack for it.

He spun back around and presented me with his creation. It was an arrowhead. "For you," he said. "Well? What do you think? Do you like it?"

"I do. Thank you, Peter." I walked outside and admired it in the sunlight. It was extra long and sharp, with a silver tip—like the ones Granny used. I'd add it to my quiver and keep it for a special occasion.

When I stepped into the clearing, I was glad to see I'd beaten everyone else to Peter's party. The image of Peter's delighted face kept my spirits high as I displayed the cake on a tree stump and wrapped a wildflower garland around its base.

Thus far, the night was working out as planned. As far as I knew, Granny was sleeping soundly at home, and—thanks to the poppy dust—none the wiser that I'd snuck out. And though the cake had settled into an odd form after traveling through the forest in my basket, it was still in one piece. I tried to keep these happy things in mind, but as I sat on a rock and smoothed out the tangles in my windblown hair, my belly knotted.

What if Granny wakes up and finds me missing?

What if Peter hates the cake?

What if no one comes to this party, and all of my lying and sneaking around was for absolutely nothing?

My thoughts were interrupted by the squeals of Violet, Florence, and Beatrice. As they paraded into the clearing in their pretty frocks and springy curls, I forced a smile. Too bad the first guests couldn't have been somebody—*anybody*—else.

"Look who's here, my dears," Violet said. "Goodness, Red, how long have you been here all alone? Bonfires never begin until nightfall. Didn't you know that?" The amusement in her brown eyes doubled when she caught sight of the cake. She closed in and circled it like a vulture. "What is *that* supposed to be?"

"It's a birthday cake," I answered. "For Peter. Well, of course it's for Peter," I amended awkwardly. "I doubt anybody else is celebrating their seventeenth birthday out here in the woods on this very night."

A snorting sound came out of Florence's pointy nose. "You brought a *cake*? What are you, his mother?"

"Oh, hush, Florence. I think it's sweet," Beatrice said, and I shot her a little smile to thank her. However, all my gratefulness vanished when she added, "Do you fancy the blacksmith's son, Red?"

"Who, me? I . . ." My cheeks felt so hot, I was sure they'd turned the color of my cloak. I stared down at my boots. "We're just friends, that's all. Friends."

"I wouldn't blame you," Beatrice whispered to me. "I think he's the most handsome boy in the whole village."

"So what happened to the cake, Red?" Violet asked, drawing our eyes back to my pastry display. "Did it fall out of your basket on the way here?"

Florence added, "And get rained on? And trampled by a bear? And beaten to a pulp with the ugly sti—?"

"That's enough, Florence. We get the picture," Violet said, pounding Florence's back. The next thing I knew, Florence was falling. As if in slow motion, her red curls splayed and her arms flew into the air. She threw her hands out to break her fall, which sent her pounding smack-dab into the middle of the cake. I watched helplessly and wordlessly as she smashed into the cake like a hammer to a pumpkin.

"Oh, my. I can be so clumsy. Look what I've done!" Florence casually licked the cake off her hands. I turned my back so they wouldn't see my blazing cheeks, but I heard the willowy redhead coughing, spitting, and carrying on. "I'm sorry to be the bearer of bad news, Red, but this cake of yours? It's even more horrid than the stone soup they force down our throats at school."

I clenched my fists and turned face-to-face with Violet. "You did that on purpose."

"It's quite unfortunate, but nothing to cry about." Violet pushed the parts of the cake together and smeared the frosting over the cracks with her fingers. "See? Good as new. And don't you worry one bit, Red. As sure as you're Widow Lucas's granddaughter, I'm certain it is *scrumptious*." She held her hand up like she was going to lick the frosting off then wiped it on my cape.

The sound of their laughter stung like tiny arrows stabbing me behind my eyes. I blinked back the tears.

"Oh, goodie. The others are arriving. Who knows, perhaps this party will finally pick up and become worthy of our presence," Violet said. "Come along, girls. We've wasted our time with Red long enough." Violet turned on her heels, and Beatrice and Florence followed her into the center of the clearing, where some boys from school had begun lighting the bonfire and torches.

Any minute, it would be dark. *Any minute, Peter will be here.* His charming grin would help me forget about Violet and her friends. But then he'd see the battered cake and wonder what had happened. What would I say? The truth, that Violet and her friends smashed it—and I didn't even do anything about it? I didn't want to confess that I was a coward, especially to Peter.

I had to do away with the cursed cake. I scooped and swept the sticky, crumbly mess into my basket and ducked into the woods. Peeking out from behind a tree from time to time, I waited quietly for a clear shot to the bonfire.

The moment I spotted Peter, my heart skipped a beat. He was wearing a clean white shirt, and though his trousers were a mite too short, I knew them to be his finest. But then Violet and the other girls swarmed him. Beatrice's words came back to me, and I wondered how many girls thought Peter was the handsomest in the village.

Was *I* one of those girls?

Shortly thereafter, Peter was sucked into the thick of a jumble of bodies, and I lost sight of him altogether. I remembered why I was hiding in the trees, and when I felt fairly certain no one was watching, I made a run for it. I opened my basket and emptied it into the flames. With a *whoosh* and a flash, the cake that had taken me hours to make melted into the flames, as if it had never existed. Up in smoke and gone, just like that. A lump lodged itself in my throat and I swallowed. What was wrong with me? It was just a stupid cake, for goodness' sake!

I bolted back to my hiding spot to gather my wits. Violet was regaling the group with one of her favorite stories of the time a gypsy gazed into a crystal ball and foresaw that it was Violet's destiny to live in a royal castle. The way everybody seemed to hang on every word—acting as if they hadn't heard her tell the same tale fifty times—both annoyed and amazed me. I had every inclination to make a mad dash home, but then I heard Peter's voice.

"Sorry to interrupt your fascinating story, Violet, but have any of you seen Red?"

"Who?" Violet asked.

"Red," he repeated. "She told me she was coming, but I haven't seen her."

When I peeked out from behind the tree, I saw Violet fluff her ebony curls. "I'm really not sure if I've seen her—or not. She's rather forgettable, don't you agree?"

I clenched my fists, wanting ever so badly to shoot an arrow just close enough to graze her stupid, perfect hair.

Peter strolled past them and asked a few others, but they shook their heads *no*.

"She was here earlier," Beatrice piped up. "Don't you remember, Violet? She baked that horrid cake that was right over . . ." She walked to the tree stump I'd used for a table. ". . . here?" Beatrice's eyes bugged out. "It's gone. And so is she!"

"Oh, Beatrice. Don't worry your pretty little head about Red. I'd wager she got hungry, gobbled down every last crumb of her cake, and ran all the way home to her granny with a terrible bellyache." Violet placed her hands on her tiny, corseted stomach and frowned.

"Wait. You're telling me that Red baked a cake?" Peter asked, sounding surprised—and, dare I say, delighted. "For me?"

Beatrice shrugged and said, "I guess. For your birthday. But like I said, it was horrid, so you're lucky it disappeared."

"And we're *all* lucky Red disappeared," Florence added.

That's it. Enough was enough. I pushed my shoulders back and held my chin up, steeling myself to march straight over to Violet and her brigade and make them eat their evil words.

Then, somewhere in the distance, a lone wolf howled. My blood ran cold. Every bit of courage instantly seeped out of me. Reduced to a mound of shivers, it was all I could do to hunker down against the tree and draw my cloak snugly around my body. I clawed at my neck, futilely searching for the golden cross. Could Granny's prediction be coming true? Were the wolves hunting already tonight?

Over by the bonfire, Beatrice flapped her arms like a fledgling. "Oh, mercy me! Did you hear that? What if the wolves got Red?"

The wolves won't harm me, I told myself. *The riding hood will keep me safe.*

"Don't be silly, Beatrice," Florence chastised. "It's not Wolfstime yet."

"But I heard a wolf howl," Beatrice said.

Violet crossed her arms over her chest and said, "Red's grandmother has the whole village on edge, but we can't stop living just because we're afraid of some overgrown mongrels."

"Speaking of Red's grandmother, my stepfather told me that the old bag is petitioning to have the Forget-Me-Not ball postponed indefinitely."

What? Why haven't I heard anything about this? No amount of swallowing would relieve my parched mouth and throat. To my mortification, Florence's announcement had perked the ears of the rest of the partygoers. "What?" and "What for?" they asked at once. They seemed as shocked as I was.

"She says it's too dangerous to have all of the village's young people in one place at the same time," Florence explained, "in case the wolves decide to hunt that night and kill every last one of us in one fell swoop."

If only Granny had told me she'd been lobbying to call off the ball, I could've tried talking some sense into her. Then again, who was I fooling to think she'd pay me any mind, especially when it came to the subject of wolves? And what would it matter anyhow, if the wolves got us tonight?

"That crazy ole bat can't cancel the ball," Beatrice said, stomping her foot. "Seamstress Evans has been working on my gown for weeks on end."

"The Forget-Me-Not ball *will* go on," Violet said firmly, and the mob pumped its fists and torches in the air and shouted in agreement. "It's been held during the Flower Moon for years, and the tradition isn't going to change just because of one crazy old lady and her granddaughter who doesn't even care about the ball because no one would want to dance with her."

From my wooded haven, I saw the bonfire surge, its flames shooting high into the night sky. The cake had vanished so easily and completely in that fire. If only the rest of my problems would disappear like that. When I heard cracks of branches and bouts of curses, I realized with mounting horror that my problems were about to get even worse.

"Do you youngsters have a death wish?" said Granny as she marched into the clearing, brandishing her trusty crossbow. Her hair flowed down to her shoulders like silver snakes, and under her shawl, her threadbare nightgown flapped in the breeze.

Oh, no. Please. No!

Five

Gasping, I rose onto my toes to get a better view of the nightmarish scene unfolding before my eyes. Why on earth is she here? How had the poppy dust lost its potency so quickly?

"Widow Lucas, what a lovely surprise," Violet said, sounding less than pleased. "I'm sure I'm speaking for us all when I say we do appreciate your concern. However, as I'm sure you can see . . ." She pointed at the sky. ". . . the moon is not full. It's not Wolfstime."

"It's full enough. The wolves are out, and the bunch of you are nothing but tasty little appetizers in their eyes. Especially *you*." She briefly pointed her weapon at a pudgy boy named Gregory Oliver. "Being out here in the forest is downright foolish! Now, if you know what's good for you, you'll scoot on home and stay there until sunrise. And you'll stay there every night all week, until Wolfstime has passed." Having said her piece, Granny lowered her weapon just a hair.

I exhaled in relief, hoping the worst was behind us. But the relief, however slight, was short-lived, because Florence stepped forward and said, "With all due respect, Widow Lucas, we have every right to be here."

I cringed, knowing that any moment, Granny would launch into one of her lectures. "Right or wrong doesn't matter one lick when you're all dead and gone, now does it!?" Granny spun around, waving her bow in the air. *What is wrong with her?* Instead of being frightened, almost everybody laughed and poked one another, seemingly thinking her behavior was hilarious. Gregory crossed his eyes and pantomimed swigging out of an invisible bottle.

Peter cautiously approached her. "Ma'am? Are you looking for your granddaughter?"

Granny pointed her bolt at him. "You. The black-smith's boy. You're the reason they're all here, putting their lives in peril."

"I'm sorry, but Red isn't here," he said, reaching over to move the arrow to the side. Unbeknownst to them, if Granny happened to pull the trigger right then and there, it would hit me square in the heart. I sidestepped, trying to get in the clear while still keeping sight of what was happening.

"She *was* here," Violet said with a shrug. "And then she left. I don't have a crystal ball or a magic mirror handy, but if I had to guess, I'd say she's prob-ably out in the deep, dark forest, wandering about all alone . . ."

"And I heard a wolf howl," Beatrice added.

The bonfire and torches cast sinister shadows on Granny's face. She started walking toward the trees, straight for me. Rather, not very straight at all. And that was when it hit me: *the poppy dust must still be in her sys-tem.* My heart stopped. I couldn't decide whether to stay perfectly still and hope against hope that she'd pass by me, or make a run for it.

"Widow Lucas, wait!" Peter called as he took off after her.

"Peter, where are you going? It's your birthday party. Let her go!" Violet shouted. A breeze blew past her, causing her hair to ripple as if each curled lock had a life of its own. I couldn't be sure, but the way she inclined her head and squinted, it seemed like Violet caught a glimpse of me. Then, the very next second, she turned on her heels and stormed back toward the bonfire, muttering something about how old fogies should leave the liquor bottles alone.

Once Peter caught up with Granny, he matched her pace. "I'll help you find your granddaughter."

"No," Granny said. "You'll only slow me down. You'll be the most help getting those fools to go back to their homes. If the wolves hunt tonight, all of the blood will be on your hands." She snatched his torch and left him standing in the clearing with his palms up and his handsome face etched with worry.

As for me, I ran along the trail and waited on a fallen log near the road. I was just about to go back for Granny when she showed up.

"Granny," I said softly.

She thrust the torch at me and then doubled over, wheezing. "Why did you run off like that? The wolf howled, and it woke me up, and when I went to your room to make sure you were all right, you were nowhere to be . . . So tired. Must . . . rest." She ungracefully plopped down on the log.

"I know. I just . . . I wanted to go to Peter's party. I knew you wouldn't allow it."

"Damn right I wouldn't allow it. I've told you a million times. You cannot go out when the wolves are hunting. Do you want to end up like your grandfather, or any one of my six brothers? Do you want to end up like your father? Like your mother?"

"No, of course not." I blinked, trying not to cry.

"Then our discussion is over." She snatched the torch from my hands and began walking fitfully toward the cottage. A dark blue cloud floated over and past the almost-full moon.

I waited a moment or two and then jogged to catch up with her. "But Granny, the wolves won't harm me. Not when I'm wearing this," I said, shaking the corner of my red riding hood for her to see. "Isn't that right?"

She sighed. "Yes. Of course. Although, when it comes to your safety, we must take every possible precaution. I can't let anything happen to you. I wouldn't be able to"—she took a deep, ragged breath—"live with myself." She sniffed, and I craned my neck to see if she was actually crying. But she turned away, so I couldn't tell. "Your friends better be on their way home."

"They're not really my friends," I said, gently taking her bow away from her. "Apart from Peter."

"Good. They're idiots. The whole lot of them. Idiots, I say."

When we finally got home, I helped Granny into her bed. The instant her head hit the pillow, she fell into a deep, snoring slumber. She looked so small in her bed, like a little girl. I brushed her hair off her face, blotted the sweat off her brow, and arranged her boots and shawl by the rocking chair. I had no idea what punishment awaited me come morning, but I had the horrible feeling it would be a doozy.

Undoubtedly, Violet and her friends would make sure everybody heard the story of Granny's raving mad intrusion, how she tottered about the forest in her night-dress and threatened everybody at Peter's party with certain death at the teeth of the wolves or the point of her arrow—whichever came first.

And this time, it really wasn't Granny's fault. It was mine.

A blanket of blackness cloaks me, and I strain to see, hear, smell, or feel something—anything at all. Finally, my ears pick something up. It's the mysterious voice that's become familiar to me: "Come."

I blindly follow the voice, feeling a gust of chilly air on my skin.

The wind blows harder, and now I'm running. The more ground I cover, the more I can make out the shapes of trees backlit by flashes of light. It becomes a game—run faster, see more. I'm amazed at how fast I'm moving.

Small woodland creatures—squirrels, mice, rabbits, and foxes—are running with me. Or at least I think they are. But an instant later, I realize they're not running with me at all. They're scattering at my feet, fleeing from me, taking cover as best they can. I feel their panic clawing mercilessly at my heart. A giant owl screeches as it shoots into the starless night sky. Its wings retract like an umbrella, revealing the perfectly round moon.

Sunday, May 13

Pots, pans, bowls, and spoons cluttered the countertops, and flour dusted everything in the kitchen—even Granny herself. "I've never seen so many muffins," I said, setting my basket of eggs on the counter. The chickens had acted even more skittish than usual, so my trip to the henhouse had taken a bit longer that morning.

Which was fine, because it gave me more time to compose myself after my terrible Wolfstime dream and steel myself for what I feared would be the lecture of my lifetime.

Granny paused just long enough to crack an egg into a bowl and then resumed stirring the batter. "Nor have I," she said.

"What are they for?" I asked, wondering why she was waiting so long to dole out my punishment. But as I studied her from a safe distance, she gave no sign that she even remembered having gone out in search of me last night.

Granny said, "That new schoolmarm of yours ordered them."

"Miss Cates?"

"That's right. She wants to treat all of her students and their families, or so the note said."

"Well, that's surprisingly generous of her," I said. "Then again, she's been acting rather giddy lately. Did you hear she's to be married to Vicar Clemmons in June?"

"It's about time someone made an honest man out of him."

"Do you truly believe those rumors? Or are you just jealous that he's thrown himself at every eligible woman in the village except for you?" I deadpanned.

She glared at me over her glasses, then asked, "What happened to your cake?"

"Oh. I, um . . . gave it to the pigs." I watched her carefully to see if she was testing me or playing some sort of game.

But she kept mixing as if nothing was amiss. "That was the sorriest cake I've seen in all my years," she said, shaking her head. "But don't worry, child. As far as your baking goes, there's nowhere to go but up. You'll get better, mark my words."

Could it be that she truly had no recollection of last night? The only explanation I could come up with was she must have been on a poppy dust–induced sleepwalk. The whole notion of her having left the house, wandered around in the forest, lectured the village young people—and even aimed her crossbow at some of them—without any recollection was downright eerie. I vowed to stay far away from poppy dust from then on.

Suddenly, Granny's face went white, and she dropped the wooden spoon in the bowl.

"What's wrong?" I asked.

She rubbed her right arm, as I'd noticed her doing many times before. "This blasted scar. It won't give me a moment's peace, not until we're done with Wolfstime. Then, next month, it'll flare up again, like clockwork."

"Wait, what?" I knew her arm ached terribly from time to time, but I just figured it was related to her old age. She'd never mentioned a scar before. "Since when do you have a scar? Can I see it?"

"Nothing to worry about."

"What's it from, then? Will you tell me that much?"

"No time for chitchat, child. I need you to go to Farmer Thompson's for milk. I've run out. Get moving, time's ticking."

I sighed. Someday, I'd get her to tell me the story

behind her scar. Maybe if I knew what caused it, I could help figure out a way to make the pain go away.

Meanwhile, I grabbed my bow and arrows and headed for the door. "Yes, Granny, I'm wearing my hood," I said before she could ask. I closed the door behind me and headed upstream to the neighbor's farm. I walked quickly, sometimes breaking into a jog. With any luck, I could carve out enough time to fetch the milk and take a quick detour to the swimming hole to search for my missing gold cross. And, with even more luck, Peter would be there in nothing but his britches. That vision certainly put a spring in my step!

Birds and dragonflies flitted about in the sky, and a frog flopped from rock to rock across the ripples of water. The forest teemed with creatures, yet they skittered away before I could get anywhere close. It wasn't always that way; there was a time when I thought they actually enjoyed my company. Though I couldn't know for sure, I wondered if the spell on my red cloak somehow repelled them in addition to protecting me from wolves.

Thank goodness, Mrs. Thompson seemed happy to see me when I knocked on the door of their cottage. "Hello, Red, what can I do for you?" she asked, rubbing her hands on her apron.

"Good afternoon, Mrs. Thompson. I need some milk. I know I was just here, but Granny is in the middle of her biggest order yet, and I'm afraid she's run out."

The farmer's wife shook her head sadly. "I'm sorry, Red, but our cow is . . . with us no more. She died just last night."

Her four-year-old daughter poked her blond head out the window and said, "Dottie got killed by a damn wolf."

Mrs. Thompson's face flushed scarlet and she uttered under her breath, "Oh, Fernie, that tongue of yours."

"A wolf?" I asked.

Mrs. Thompson sighed. "She overheard her pa sayin' that, yes. So I suppose it's true. Pity, too. Dottie was a good cow."

"An' we needed the milk money to pay the damn

tax man," said the girl, adding to her mother's apparent chagrin.

"Fernie, *language*," she scolded her daughter. "My apologies, Red. She might look just like me, but that mouth of hers is all her father's. Funny how the apple don't fall far from the tree."

"It's all right, Mrs. Thompson. If you think colorful language bothers me, you haven't met my grandmother."

The farmer's wife chuckled and nodded understandingly.

"I'm sorry to hear about your cow."

"Thank you, Red. Sorry we can't help you with the milk. Have you tried the Roberts's place, up the stream a bit further?"

I swallowed, trying to get the lump out of my throat. I knew the Roberts family had cows, but their youngest daughter, Violet, was the last person I wanted to see.

Six

February, three years ago

"How many do you need?" Granny asked as she lined my basket with a freshly washed and ironed cloth in a blue, red, and white plaid.

Of course, I knew the answer straightaway; but there was something exciting about saying their names out loud. I counted on my fingers, "Violet, Beatrice, and Florence. And *me*."

"You realize these gooseberry tarts won the blue ribbon at the village bake-off."

Oh, I knew. That's precisely why I chose to bring them. It wasn't every day Violet and her friends asked an outsider to their winter picnic, and this was the first time they'd delivered an invitation to me. The invitation itself was so exquisite—paper white as snow, ink black as coal, and written in Violet's enviably artistic hand—I'd displayed it on my bedroom mirror and counted down the seven days as if it were for Christmas. Only the finest treat would do for such a momentous occasion. I wanted them to remember the day they'd included me in their winter picnic.

"Make sure you're back well before sunset," Granny said, stacking the tarts in the basket with great care.

"I will. Thank you, Granny. I'm sure my friends will love them." Referring to Violet, Beatrice, and Florence as "friends" might have been a stretch. *But who knows?* Maybe if I made a good impression, they would truly want me to join their circle.

"Of course, they'll love them," Granny said brusquely. "That goes without saying. The king himself would demand I keep his dessert table full—if he'd only get off his high horse long enough to sink his teeth into one of these little masterpieces." She gripped the tart in her hand so hard it busted in two. Shrugging, she stuffed half into her mouth and half into mine.

"Mmmm. Oh, Granny, you've outdone yourself," I said while chewing.

I started toward the front door, until Granny reminded me, "Your hood!"

I rushed to my room and took the red cloak off my bedpost, stealing a glance at myself in the mirror to make sure my braids hadn't frayed. I gave my cheeks a quick pinch and smiled at my reflection in the looking glass. "What a wonderful day for a picnic," I whispered to myself. "The first of many."

"Good-bye, Granny," I called before heading out. "I won't be long."

"Take your time, child."

Fresh snow covered the road, and droplets of ice twinkled in the sunlight like tiny stars. I almost felt bad leaving boot prints in the pristine blanket of white. A hare hopped alongside me for a little while, and then a squirrel kept me company with its nonstop chatter. I turned off the road and cut into the forest, and was pleased to see three sets of boot prints, all heading toward the secret spot described in the invitation as "where the stream meets the white oak tree that was struck by lightning."

I was sure I knew precisely the spot, and I smiled when I glimpsed a little table all set up with a tablecloth, cups and plates, and four wooden chairs. Sprigs of holly crisscrossed the length of the table, and the whole effect was lovely, like a Christmas tea party in one of my old storybooks. I couldn't believe my good fortune to be included.

Where is everybody? Out of the corner of my eye, I thought I saw somebody dressed in red, standing in the middle of the small clearing. On second glance, I could tell it wasn't a person after all; it was a snowman. Only this snowman wasn't the usual type, with coal eyes, a carrot nose, and a scarf. He—or she, I should say—wore a red tablecloth draped over her head and flowing down her back. A snow-girl wearing a red-hooded cloak.

It was, I realized at once, supposed to be me.

Rustling noises came from behind some bushes. I whirled around, and a snowball exploded on my left cheek. The hit stung my bare skin. I thought I felt blood, but when I touched my face, a smear of mud stained my mitten. More snowballs pelted me from the opposite direction. I ducked and dodged for a moment or two, and then collapsed onto my knees, where the snowballs and laughter hit me from every direction, coating me in mud and humiliation. I stayed in that position, my cloak protecting my skin from the stings, until finally the torture stopped. I lifted my hood just enough to peer out.

"Enough fun and games," Violet said, appearing in the open. "I'm completely bored. And famished."

"Oh, goodie! It's time for the picnic!" Beatrice said. "Come on, Red. Get up." I tried to hold my shoulders steady, so they couldn't tell that I was sobbing. "Red? Are you all right?"

Florence said, "She's fine, just fine. She's just resting, Beatrice. Anyone can see that."

"I hope she doesn't rest too long," Beatrice said. "I've worked up quite an appetite."

"I'm sure she won't mind if we begin without her," Florence said, but Violet did not approve.

"Florence, I'm surprised at you. Red is our special guest. She told everyone that she wanted to be included in our winter picnic, and here she is—a dream come true for her, I'm sure. We won't start until she's good and ready."

A scrawny squirrel skittered across the snow. He stood on his hind legs and clicked, and another squirrel joined him as they prodded my basket. With my mitten, I wiped the tears away and slowly stood.

"Oh, my goodness, Red. You're a mess," said Violet. "But we don't mind. Come on over here and join us." It took everything I had not to hurl my basket at her. Instead, I brushed the mud and snow off of myself as well as possible and then kicked the snow-girl down, leaving a shapeless mound beneath the red cloth.

"That wasn't very nice," said Florence. "That snow-man took us half an hour to make for you."

"So I take it you don't want to come to our next winter picnic?" Beatrice asked.

"I guess you're not quite as stupid as everybody says you are," I said.

The walk home seemed twice as long as the walk to their picnic spot. Maybe it was because I kept pausing to feed the two squirrels and other woodland critters Granny's prized gooseberry tarts—a generous eight instead of the four I'd asked for.

"I'm home, Granny," I announced, yanking my feet out of my dirty boots.

"This is earlier than expected," she said. "To what do I owe the pleasure?" She looked up from her knitting and dropped her needles in her lap. "Goodness gracious, child! What the dickens happened to you?"

"I fell," I lied. "I'm just an oaf, I suppose."

Granny adjusted her glasses. "I'll say! You look like you took a dive in the pigsty. Now that you're thirteen, you should probably roll around in the mud a bit less and act more like a lady." She gathered her knitting and piled it neatly on the stool. Then she stood, using the arm of the sofa for support. "Here, hand me that hood. I'll get it washed up, good as new."

"Thank you, Granny."

She took my basket from me and set it on the coffee table while I shed my cloak. "I take it your girlfriends enjoyed the tarts?" she asked.

I stared down at my stockinged feet. "I don't think they're very fond of me."

"Oh? Why do you say that?"

"They made a snowman . . ." I started to tell her what had happened, but the look of worry—with a spark of anger—in her eyes made me reconsider. I didn't want to upset her. She was scary when she got really upset.

Besides, now that it was over, I wasn't so sure that what Violet, Beatrice, and Florence did was intentionally cruel. Maybe their idea of fun and games was quite different than mine, and that's why I got along best with boys. "Never mind, it's nothing."

She waited, probably to see if I'd change my mind and tell her the story after all, but when I wordlessly handed over my cloak, she said, "The best of friendships don't happen overnight, child. They'll grow to adore you; you'll see. You'll just have to be patient."

I sighed. "I wish I could go to the wizard and get a friendship spell."

"*No*, you don't." The graveness of her tone startled me, and I stood at attention.

"Yes, I do. You did it for my riding hood, only for a protection spell, right?"

"Yes; however, magic always comes with a price. You might think you want something, and that magic is the only way; but more times than not, it ends up costing yourself or your loved ones in ways you cannot even begin to fathom. Even when magic is used for good, it can become something very bad."

I wasn't quite sure I followed, but I nodded anyhow.

She folded my muddy cloak in two and hugged it to her bosom, which made me worry that she'd have to wash her blouse, too. "Those girls will come around sooner or later, mark my words."

The Roberts family lived near the fork in the stream, in one of the nicest cottages in the whole village. Mrs. Roberts hosted gatherings every few weeks, whether or not she could name an occasion worthy of celebrating. With Violet's eldest sister at the piano and their father's pitch-perfect baritone, they entertained the villagers, who enjoyed singing, clapping, and dancing for hours after they'd cleaned their plates and emptied their glasses.

Most people found Mrs. Roberts's get-togethers charming and made every effort to be in attendance, but Granny found the parties altogether loathsome, complaining that Mrs. Roberts only adored being adored. "It would save that woman a lot of time and money if she'd just sit in front of her mirror and tell her reflection how wonderful she is," Granny always said. Granny had made up excuses to miss the parties so often the invitations eventually stopped coming.

I never really minded, because it gave me extra time to practice shooting arrows or to swim with Peter and the boys, which is what I wished I was doing right then. I inhaled, exhaled, and rapped on the door.

From inside, I heard Mrs. Roberts holler, "Violet, be a lamb and see who's here. I just have two more rows to finish."

I took another deep breath and hoped Violet wouldn't notice the beads of sweat on my forehead.

"Red? What are you doing here?" Violet asked when she opened the door.

"I was hoping I could buy some milk."

She raised her left eyebrow and tilted her head. "Is that so? Well, I suppose that could be arranged."

"Miss Cates made a large order," I couldn't resist saying. I knew she thought my granny was as mad as a hatter, and now a drunkard as well, so I wanted her to know that Granny's baked goods were very much in demand. "We've barely been able to keep up with all the baking and deliveries—and it's all we can do to keep enough ingredients on hand. Granny's business is doing very well, you know."

"Well, I do now," Violet said, twirling one of her dark curls around her finger. "Good for her." I didn't want to hear about how Granny had crashed the bonfire party with her mighty crossbow. Or about how Granny was scheming to get the Forget-Me-Not ball canceled. The quicker I could procure the milk and get away from Violet, the better.

Violet gestured for me to follow her inside, and I did. Someone—most likely one of her sisters—was playing the piano in the music hall, and when we entered the living room, Mrs. Roberts glanced up from her sewing.

"Red, is that you?" Mrs. Roberts asked. Her hair was every bit as thick and long as Violet's, yet streaks of white lightened her temples. "My, you've been growing like a beanstalk. Skinny as one, too. Is that grandmother of yours feeding you enough, dear?"

"Red has come for some milk, Mother," said Violet. "Do we have any to spare?"

"I believe we do," Mrs. Roberts answered. "Once I get to a good stopping point, I'll go and check. In the meantime, why don't you take a seat, Red? I'm sure you girls have plenty to chat about. I overheard Violet telling her sisters what a nice time she had at last night's bonfire. I'm sure you did, as well."

"Yes, but it's too bad you had to leave so early," Violet said. "And it's too bad what happened to the lovely cake you brought."

"Oh?" Mrs. Roberts set her needlepoint on the armrest of the sofa. "What happened to it?"

Digging my fingernails into the tapestry of the chair I sat in, I said, "Florence smashed it."

"Goodness me." Violet chuckled. "That's the truth, but of course it was a most unfortunate accident. She tripped and fell onto it. She felt horrible about it. It's all the poor, clumsy girl talked about all night long: how terrible she felt."

"And you played a part in it, as well, Violet," I reminded her.

She chuckled again. "I sure did, Mother. I tried to put the cake back together using my own two hands."

"That's my precious little lamb." Mother and daughter shared a sickeningly sweet moment that made me shudder. Finally, Mrs. Roberts excused herself to go check on the milk.

Violet crossed the room and opened the window, probably to rid the room of the stench of dishonesty. I was thankful for the fresh air, but I wished Mrs. Roberts would hurry. I couldn't stand being in that house or anywhere near Violet. With each passing second, I wished I had never come. If only there had been another way to get the milk Granny needed.

"So, I'm sure you're eager to hear what all happened at Peter's party after you left," Violet said.

"All right," I agreed, against my best instincts. I couldn't leave without what I came for, and because of that, I couldn't risk acting cross—especially since we hadn't negotiated a price, and I might not have had enough in my pouch.

Violet leaned on the curio, her shiny black boots reflecting rays of sunlight. "Gregory pulled out his fiddle, and before you knew it, everyone was dancing round the bonfire. It was delightful."

That did sound nice, I had to admit. "Oh?"

"I took a spin with Peter—it was his birthday, after all—and what better gift than a dance with me?"

"Oh." My stomach roiled. I couldn't bear to remain sitting, so I walked over to the window, hoping to see Mrs. Roberts on her way back from the barn with the milk. But sadly, the only creature in the path was a starling, pecking at an insect or worm in the dirt.

Violet continued, "You wouldn't believe it if you didn't see it, but Peter can dance. The other girls saw it, too, and one by one they asked him to dance with them. One by one, he turned them away. He danced with me and only me. I guess I must have been caught up in the excitement of it all—the fire, the music, the dancing bodies all around me, the big, silver moon—and when Peter asked me to save him the first dance at the Forget-Me-Not ball . . ." The song her sister was playing on the piano came to an abrupt end. As the muffled sound of rustling papers came from the music hall, Violet pressed her lips together and widened her eyes. ". . . I said yes!"

My jaw dropped. It was too late to try to disguise my shock. "I didn't realize he fancied you." I held my hand up to my mouth, silently chastising myself for letting that slip out, and before they'd given me a price for the milk. "What I meant to say is I'm quite sure he's never mentioned it, not even once."

"Who knows? Perhaps he's only recently fallen under my spell." She paused a moment and then laughed as if a private memory had tickled her mind. "That tends to happen when they kiss me."

My knees went to mush, like they'd forgotten how to hold my weight. I reminded myself that Peter and I were friends, nothing more—but I hated the very thought of him kissing somebody else. Especially if that somebody was Violet Roberts.

"You're lying," I choked out. "You're nothing but a liar."

"Am I?" Her rosy lips curved up. "My dear Red, if you

only knew me better, you'd realize I never lie. Lying is unbecoming. Still, if you don't believe me, perhaps you should ask your friend Peter to fill in the story for you."

I wanted to say, "Oh, I will," but my throat closed up, barely allowing me to breathe, let alone speak.

Once Mrs. Roberts returned, she said, "It's our lucky day!" and held a jug up in the air as triumphantly as a hunter holds a rabbit.

"Thank you," I managed to croak. "How much do I owe you?" Averting my eyes from Violet's glare, I dug into my pouch. My hands were shaking, so it took me an excruciatingly long time to gather the coins.

"Red? Your face is ghastly pale. Are you not feeling well?" asked Mrs. Roberts.

"I've never been better," I lied.

"Well. Today, you owe nothing. It's on the house." Mrs. Roberts frowned. "Maybe you should go home and rest, dear girl. You really do look like you're coming down with something. And please, try to put some meat on those bones of yours." The way she said the last part made me think of the story of the witch who made a house of candy in the hopes of snaring children to feast upon.

"No, really. I have the money. Please, Mrs. Roberts, take it."

I held the coins for her, but she shook her head and said, "Red, it's no secret that your grandmother is . . . How do I put this delicately? Not very stable right now. Please, accept our offering. It is our hope that it helps you both in your unfortunate . . . situation."

My eyes flickered over to Violet, whose lips were pursed like she was trying to hold back a huge grin. It felt as if someone had just forced a cupful of salt down my throat. "There is no 'situation,' Mrs. Roberts," I said, finally. "We're fine. Actually, I was telling Violet when I first arrived that Granny's baking business is doing very well."

Mrs. Roberts lifted her chin and arched an eyebrow, and she appeared every bit the older version of Violet. "Now, Red. Don't be disrespectful. Take our gift."

I bit back a grimace. Taking the proffered jug, I mumbled, "Thank you," then turned on my heels. Before dashing into the woods, I placed the coins in a pile on their stoop. I couldn't get out of Violet's house fast enough. Though I knew my mind had to be tricking me, I heard her cruel laughter and felt her searing stare even after I'd slipped well out of her view.

Seven

As I marched down the road, I squeezed the jug with all my might, giving it a punishing death grip. How could Peter have asked the meanest, vilest, most wretched girl in the village for the first dance at the Forget-Me-Not ball? Had I been only imagining it when he and I'd agreed to go to the swimming hole instead of the stupid, pretentious ball?

How could he have *kissed* her?

I thought he had more sense than that—as well as taste and dignity. I could go on and on about all the reasons Peter should stay away from Violet. I'd never told anybody about the red-hooded snow-girl in the forest, but I truly believed that Peter and I were on the same page about how Violet and her devoted duo might be fair on the outside, but were rotten on the inside, all the way to the core. I longed for the comfort my cross necklace brought me at times like this, when I felt so alone.

But then again, I didn't feel alone. I couldn't quite explain it, but I had the strong sensation that someone— or some*thing*—was watching me.

The sun had started its descent in the west, and a heavy fog had rolled in, blurring the forest into hazy, unfamiliar shapes. Though I fought against it, my mind wandered to the wolves.

A branch snapped. I stopped in my tracks and pricked up my ears, listening for anything out of the ordinary. My ears filled with the strangest sound of anything I could imagine for a bustling forest: *silence*. Not even a rodent scuttling, a bat's wings flapping, or a leaf rustling in the wind. For an eerie moment, the world stood still.

I turned just a hair and spotted a pair of huge amber-colored eyes. They had to belong to a wolf, and suddenly, my blood ran cold. The eyes gleamed at me from the hollow between a towering spruce and a tangle of scrubs. Though I didn't dare move a muscle, I closed my eyes and focused on my red riding hood. *It will protect me always*, I recited in my mind. Granny promised it would.

I waited, hearing only the pounding of my heart. The pounding grew louder, like someone was beating drums inside my ribs. Finally, questioning if what I thought I'd seen were eyes at all—or just a cruel joke my imagination was playing on me—I took a second look.

This time, there was nothing but a dark, empty shadow. *It was probably just your imagination*, I told myself. I concentrated on my breathing for what seemed like forever. When nothing out of the ordinary happened, I started walking home again, placing one scuffed boot in front of the other. The usual noises of the woods resumed. But the instant I started feeling safe, I heard something behind me—footsteps falling on the forest floor. They were faster than mine, and I could tell that each covered more ground.

My legs seemed to have a mind of their own, and before I knew it, I was running.

"You will never outrun it. Your only hope is to hide. Hide, child." The words echoed in my mind, the voice all too familiar. But it wasn't the voice I'd heard in my dreams. It was Granny's.

The footsteps sounded close, too close. My time was up. I squeezed my eyes shut. "I'm sorry, Granny," I whispered, hoping the breeze would bring my last words to her. I owed Granny so many apologies, at least a thousand for each of the sixteen years she'd spent raising me.

On second thought, I wanted my final words to be something more poignant, something she could hold on to for the rest of her time. "I love you, Granny," I whispered ever so softly. It occurred to me that I hadn't said those words in a long while. Too long.

I whirled around, steeling myself to face my fate. I expected my frightened gaze to be trounced by a pair of wild, bloodthirsty eyes. I was ready to flinch, scream, collapse. Die.

But all I saw was forest. Endless acres of soaring trees. Leaves clinging to their branches as if for dear life, while others twirled down to the fern-covered floor with each breath of the evening wind. Bright green moss and lichens splotched the rocks and tree trunks. Ordinary, familiar, harmless.

Whatever was chasing me had to be invisible, or at least very well camouflaged. Perhaps it was nothing at all. Or maybe I was going mad, like so many people believed Granny was. But then I heard it again: thumping and bumping. Still, inexplicably, nothing emerged from the woods, not even a mouse.

I started running. Shielding my face with one arm and gripping the jug of milk with the other, I burst through a thicket. The prickly twigs clawed at my cloak. Roots tripped me like dozens of angry elves. I caught myself on a gigantic oak tree, but its moss-covered trunk buckled beneath my hand, and I dropped the jug. Before I could right it, the last drops of milk soaked into the thirsty earth.

"Hide," Granny's voice repeated in my aching head.

A hole appeared in the tree, swallowing me into its hollow haven. Like magic, a curtain of dried-up vines swung over the opening. As they swished back into place, they whispered, *Shhhh.*

It was the perfect hiding place, and I thanked my lucky stars to have fallen into it, even if I'd spilled the milk getting there. But I knew better than to assume myself safe. Safer, yes. But completely safe, never.

I wrapped the cloak snugly around my body and adjusted the hood so it shrouded my face. I shrank into its red, velvety folds, believing in its power. It seemed the more I told myself to trust in it, the more questions threatened my faith. What if the cloak wasn't magic at all, like the feather in that story Granny used to tell to me about the elephant with the big ears? What if it was just a hoax, like the tale about the emperor who was conned into thinking that he was decked in the finest clothes in the land, only to discover that he'd been parading around completely naked?

What if, when faced with razor-sharp teeth and a thirst for human blood, the cloak was just a cover for a trembling, insecure girl without a hope?

If it wanted me, all it needed to do was track me down. My boot prints and my scent would give me away as sure as the moon would be full that night.

It was so close; I heard its every breath: inhale, exhale, inhale.

This cannot be how it ends. I haven't had my happy ending. I haven't even had my first kiss!

"Red? Red! Where are you?"

Peter?

I swept the curtain of vines aside and peered out. Grayish-green fog curled into the haven, billowing at my feet and flanking my skirts. Beyond the bushes, I spotted something, and with the shifting of shadows and mist, I could just make out his silhouette.

It *was* Peter! Relief flooded each and every part of my body.

"Peter!" On wobbly legs, I stepped out of the tree.

"Red! There you are. You scared me."

"*I* scared *you?*" I countered, and then thought twice about confessing that he'd frightened me to the point where I'd imagined my grandmother talking to me and said my final words to her. "Why are you chasing me?"

"I have something of yours." He reached in his pocket and placed something small and cold in my palm. It was my gold cross! "I was just over yonder at our pond and found it. Then I happened to see you—well, your red cloak, anyhow—walking through the woods."

"Oh, Peter. Thank you!" I said, brimming with grate-fulness. Letting the chain dangle through my fingers, I ran my thumb over the familiar smoothness of the golden cross. As my finger and thumb framed the pen-dant, it seemed to beam at me, glad to be back where it belonged.

"Oh, it was nothin'. But you gave me an impressive chase, I must admit." He chuckled, despite himself. "I thought I'd never catch you."

I said, "Had I known it was you, I would never have

allowed such a thing," and Peter just grinned and kicked a pebble. When our eyes met, I saw something foreign and exciting—yet also familiar and true—in his big brown eyes. I felt like I had when I'd jumped off the rock at the swimming hole. The strange and wonderful desire to kiss Peter hit me full force. Would it be so awful? I wondered what it would feel like, and silently cursed Violet for knowing.

I was sick of Violet ruining everything for me. *I won't allow her to steal this moment.* I stepped closer to Peter until the tips of our boots touched. "Will you be so kind as to put it on for me?" I handed him my mother's necklace and then twirled around. Moving the hood of my cloak to the side, I lifted my long, dark hair.

As he latched the necklace, his breath tickled the back of my neck. It felt warm against my skin, and yet it gave me goose bumps.

"Here, let's see how it looks." He twirled me back around, and his eyes rose from the cross up to my face. I had to be blushing something awful; it felt like there was an invisible torch between us. "Beautiful," he said softly.

I cleared my throat. "Um, thank you."

"My pleasure."

"I'm sorry I left your party so early," I blurted into the silence that followed. "I had to get home."

"I was worried. But I went home by way of your cottage. The candles in your bedroom were lit, and I could see your silhouette."

"Oh," I said, not sure what to think. On one hand, I was happy to know he cared about my welfare. On the other, I hoped he hadn't seen me clearly, because I hadn't worn a nightgown for an entire week! With the mere thought of Peter seeing me undressed, I was sure I blushed the hue of my riding hood. *I'll never sleep in only my underthings again*, I vowed.

Peter tugged his ear and dropped his gaze to the ground. "I'm not a Peeping Tom or anything, I just wanted to make sure you were home. I was glad to see that you were safe." A few seconds later, his eyes met mine. "Though I must admit," he continued, "I felt slighted when I heard you'd brought me a birthday cake, and I never got even a bite of it."

"I'm sorry. Maybe I'll make one for your next birthday." *Better yet, I'll ask Granny to.*

"So, where are you off to in such a rush, anyway?" he asked, kicking rocks again.

"My grandmother asked me to fetch some milk for her, but it hasn't exactly gone as planned . . ." I retrieved the jug and held it upside down to show it was completely dry. "She needs it for her baking."

"And so she shall have it," Peter said, swooping up the jug. "Lucky for you, I can fill this empty vessel with milk. All it takes is a little magic. Come on!"

Peter took me to his house and made me wait in the stable. He took the jug and disappeared, only to return with it a few minutes later. "And with a snap of my fingers, the milk your granny needs will appear in the jug!" he said with gusto that rivaled the puppeteer at market.

"Like magic?" I played along.

"Not *like* magic, Red. It *is* magic." Peter snapped his fingers.

On cue, I peered into the "magically" filled jug. "Oh, Peter, thank you. I could just kiss you!" Even before the squeaking, smacking "kissing" noises wafted down to us from the loft, my cheeks burned with embarrassment. "But not really," I amended, while our audience of pint-sized boys carried on. "I would never *actually* kiss you."

"Whew, that's a relief," Peter said, loud enough for his brothers to hear.

They sniggered even louder when Peter hoisted me up onto his white-and-gray horse and accidentally—or perhaps *not* accidentally?—touched my bottom. My face blazed even as the mare broke into a gallop, leaving the rascals far behind.

At first, I sat rigidly behind Peter, holding on to him only tight enough to keep from falling or dropping the milk jug. It occurred to me that Peter had given me what was likely a whole day's ration for his family, and his generosity and goodness warmed my soul.

"Let's go faster," I said once we'd made it to the road. Peter gave his horse a kick and she broke into a run. I knew he probably thought I needed to get home as quickly as possible—and that much was true. But the main reason I wanted to pick up speed was so I'd have an excuse to hug myself tightly against his body.

I breathed in the scent of him: leather, wood, metal, and soap. I never tired of that smell, and I doubted I ever would.

If he had kissed Violet—and I wished with all my might that he hadn't—she didn't deserve him. "Don't take me all the way home," I warned him when I realized we were almost to the cottage. "Granny will come unraveled if she knows I've been out and about with you . . ." He probably knew, but I felt bad telling him outright that Granny didn't trust him—or any teenaged boy, for that matter—so I added, "when I have so much work to do."

"And it's less than an hour before sunset," Peter said with a nod. "The whole village knows how serious your grandmother is about Wolfstime." He tugged the reins, and after his horse came to a stop, he held the jug for me until I hopped down.

I reached up for the milk, but before letting go, he said, "Careful now. I hear you have a dreadful milk-spilling problem."

I gave him a courtesy chuckle, and after we said our good-byes, he rode away, disappearing over the hill. As I walked up the path to the cottage, I hoped it wouldn't be long until I got to see Peter again.

The door swung open before I'd even reached the porch. Granny stood in the entry, her hands on her hips, glaring at me over the rim of her glasses. I immediately wiped the smile off my mug. "Where have you been?" she demanded. "Can't you see it's almost dark?"

"Sorry, Granny. I know you've been waiting for the milk."

"I don't give a turkey gizzard about the damned milk. It's *you* I'm worried about."

"A wolf killed Farmer Thompson's cow last night, so I

had to fetch milk over at the Roberts's place. I'm sorry I made you worry. It just took longer than expected."

She looked over my shoulder, into the ever-darkening woods, and visibly shuddered. "Get your tail feathers in this house and help me get ready for Wolfstime."

Eight

I am afraid to move, and yet I am starving for air.
What will become of me when I give in? Wind and rain mercilessly
lash out at my body, and I have no choice but to bend. My body
bows and twists until I hear the noise of a twig breaking. Twigs
seem to be snapping all around me and inside of me. Twigs, branches,
bones. I collapse to the ground, gasping for air, but filling my lungs
with dirt and pebbles instead.

And then I hear the voice. "Don't fight, just be."

I breathe deeply, my throat searing in pain as air forces the dirt
out of my body and back into the earth.

Monday, May 14

The night had been largely uneventful. Granny had baked muffins deep into the wee hours, but she'd insisted that I got a good night's sleep. I wasn't sure if she really wanted me to be bright-eyed for school, or if she simply wanted me out of her kitchen so I wouldn't somehow ruin the muffins just by being there. I'd fallen asleep without any problem. Still, my eyes felt and looked far from bright when I awoke.

I remembered little of the dream I'd had, but an undeniable sense of fear lingered even as I made the daily trek across the backyard for eggs. I spotted a paw print in the dirt just outside the chicken coop and gasped. The print was about eight or nine inches across with big, long claws. Much larger and more ferocious-looking than an ordinary wolf's. My heart banged in my chest as I forced myself to push open the door. I dropped the basket in the dirt and stood frozen among clumps of brown and white feathers, bits and pieces of chicken, and blood.

"Granny! Come quick!" I screamed. My stomach

lurched, and when I swallowed, I tasted bitter bile. I clenched my eyes until I heard the clomping of Granny's boots on the path.

"What is it, child? What's all the fuss about?" Granny arrived huffing and puffing, trying to catch her breath. Of course, I didn't need to answer, because the terrible massacre lay before her eyes. Waving her hands, she stumbled as she stepped back. "Oh, no. No, no, no."

"It's so awful! How could it do this? How could it kill all of our chickens like this?"

Granny ushered me out and shut the door behind us. "I'll clean it up when you're at school. Try not to think about it."

"But . . ." What, did she think I could erase it from my mind, like it had never happened?

"Come back inside. I have the muffins all packed for you to deliver to Miss Cates. The money we'll make from this order will get us some more chickens at market this afternoon. See? It will all work out."

I wanted to believe the words Granny had delivered

so brightly and assuredly, and yet her hands were trembling, and her face had already turned a sickly white.

As soon as I arrived at school, I could not wait to hand off the muffins. For one thing, my basket was horribly heavy; for another, I hoped that once I had Miss Cates's payment and could replace our chickens, things would be back to normal for Granny and me in no time.

"Miss Cates, wait!" I called when I spotted her passing the climbing tree. I caught up with her and opened the basket lid. "Here's your order of muffins, as promised."

As usual, the small, birdlike woman wore her light blond hair pulled into a bun that perched on the top of her head, but today she'd tucked a white blossom into the side of it. She peeked into the basket and said, "They're lovely, and I'm sure every bit as delicious as they smell. But I'm sorry, Red. I didn't order any muffins." She chuckled softly before rambling on. "That's a bit extravagant for anyone I'd think, especially for somebody who's saving every last penny for her upcoming wed—"

"I'm sorry, what did you say?" I asked. Some younger girls were singing a jump rope ditty at the side of the schoolhouse, so it was possible I hadn't heard her correctly. I *must* have misheard.

"Your grandma probably mixed me up with someone else. Mix-ups happen, you know. Especially when we grow older." Miss Cates raised her eyebrows sympathetically and handed back the muffins. Somehow my basket felt even heavier than when I'd schlepped it all the way to school.

"She specifically said they were for you," I insisted. "It wasn't a mistake. Granny might not be a spring chicken—" Oh, why had I used *that* particular expression, when the horror of finding our massacred chickens was all too fresh? And if Miss Cates said she hadn't made the order, certainly she wasn't planning on paying for it. Where would we get the money to buy new chickens? "—but she's sharp as the tip of an arrow."

When I thought about all the time and ingredients Granny wasted on the muffins—never mind my most unpleasant trip to Violet's house for milk—I shook my head in confusion and disappointment.

What went wrong? Was Miss Cates lying?

No, of course not. Why would my teacher lie about a muffin order?

I hated to entertain the idea, even as a teensy possibility, but could Granny be losing her marbles?

Miss Cates's thin lips formed a gentle smile. "Why, of course your grandmother is sharp. I didn't mean anything by that. I truly am sorry, Red. I'm certain you'll be able to sell the muffins at market. Now, I need to tend to some tasks in the schoolhouse before the day officially commences. If you'll excuse me . . ."

I picked up the awful sound of Violet, Beatrice, and Florence's laughter from behind the little gray building, where the oldest boys were playing horseshoes. The girls were too far away to have heard anything, so they couldn't be sniggering at me—but for some reason, it felt like it. Their laughter waxed as they crossed over to me.

I didn't know what they wanted, and I wasn't about to stick around and find out. Turning my back to them, I started climbing the steps.

Violet grabbed my shoulder. "What's in the basket, Red? Are those the muffins you said Miss Cates ordered?" she asked. "Why didn't she take them, then?"

I wriggled out of Violet's hold and tried to think of something to say—anything that would make sense without letting on that my granny might be slipping. Then it struck me: at Violet's house, I'd mentioned that Miss Cates had made an order, but I never said that she'd specifically requested *muffins*. Either Violet had jumped to that conclusion on her own, or—and I clenched the basket tighter as the revelation struck me—Violet Roberts had everything to do with the "mix-up."

Forcing myself to smile pleasantly, as if nothing was wrong, I flipped open the basket lid. Beatrice's eyes widened and I could all but see her mouth watering. I cleared my throat and held up my chin, hoping my forthcoming lie would sound completely convincing. "Oh, no, Violet. These aren't for Miss Cates. I was merely asking her permission to give these muffins out to our classmates as samples."

"You mean, for free?" Florence raised her left eyebrow skeptically. "Why would she do that? Doesn't she have taxes to pay, like the rest of our parents?"

"Yes, Florence, for free," I said. "My granny is very generous." *Generous enough to offer me to a dragon at suppertime, once she finds out I'm giving away her baked goods.*

Beatrice and Florence lunged forward, clearly wanting a go at the treats, but Violet held her arms out, holding them back. Violet pulled a face as if she was trying to do a difficult arithmetic problem in her mind—or even a simple one, for that matter. "Red, I think you must be confused," she said. "When you were at my house looking for milk, and my charitable mother gave you some out of the kindness of her heart, I could have sworn you said Miss Cates ordered a bunch of muffins."

"I never said Miss Cates ordered a single muffin. Plus,

the milk I used for these delicious morsels came from Peter, not your mother. It seems you're the one who's confused, Violet."

Violet narrowed her eyes at me as Beatrice and Florence pushed past her arms.

"They do look delicious," Beatrice agreed. "May I?"

It was almost time for Miss Cates to ring the bell, and as the schoolchildren made their way into the yard, they paused to see why Violet and her two best friends had flocked to me and my basket. "My granny is the best baker in the village," I said, loud enough for all to hear. "And today, she's decided to give you all free samples. There are plenty of muffins to go around. Help yourself, and remember to tell your families how delicious Granny's baked goods are," I said, holding a muffin beneath Beatrice's sniffing nose. "Tell your parents to get their orders in as soon as possible, because there's sure to be a waiting list!"

As Violet's two closest friends seemed to relish every bite of their samples, I recalled all the times that Granny had rubbed her aching arm. Violet's malicious prank hadn't only been a waste of time and ingredients; the extra baking had worsened Granny's pain. I clutched the basket in anger, wishing that Granny had baked poison into her muffins.

"Oh, that's an excellent plan," Violet said, standing in the way of me handing out the samples. "I really do hope your granny gets hordes of new customers. Because let's face it, Red; you sure could use a new pair of boots."

"Oh, it will work just fine," I said, and then took the entire top off a muffin with one very big, unladylike bite.

Miss Cates slipped outside and rang the bell. "Time for class," she called. "Don't tarry, students. We have much to learn today." Everybody rushed up the school-house steps, and those who hadn't had a go at a free sample grumbled and moaned. "You will have your chance to enjoy one of the Widow Lucas's muffins after school," Miss Cates promised. "Red, please leave your basket out here. Otherwise, I'm afraid it will only be a distraction." I only nodded, as my mouth was impossibly full. She took a blueberry muffin for herself and filed into the little stone building behind the last of her students, apart from Peter, who was clearly trying to slip in before our teacher realized he'd only just arrived.

"Peter! You're tardy again," I chided him. "Do you get your chuckles out of having to wear the dunce hat?"

He swept his hair out of his eyes and smiled at me. "Oh, come on, Red. I know you think I look quite dapper in it."

Well, he kind of did. Then again, I thought he always looked adorable. I wasn't going to tell *him* that, though. "Here, have a muffin," I said instead.

"What's the occasion? My un-birthday? And what in the land happened to *that* one?"

I'd forgotten about the half-muffin in my hand. "Oh, right. I ate the top off. Here, have a whole one."

I held my basket out for Peter to make his selection, but he took the first muffin I'd offered. "I'd much rather this one."

I set the basket down and followed him inside. I was

so absorbed in trying to keep from blushing while he ate my leftovers that it took me a moment or two to feel the heat of Violet's stare from the front of the room. As I scooted to my desk, I gave her a little wave, and she turned her back to me, her curls glistening in the sunlight as they bounced perfectly into place. I didn't know how, but I wanted Violet to suffer for what she'd done to my grandmother.

I was relieved when Miss Cates announced that it was time to work on writing because arithmetic was giving me a headache, and also, it meant the school day was almost over. We wiped our slates clean, and while we waited for further instructions, Florence raised her hand. "Florence, do you have a question?" Miss Cates asked.

"Yes, ma'am. May I please be excused to use the loo?"

"I'll be dismissing class in twenty minutes. Can't you wait?"

Florence shook her head *no*, and a twelve-year-old named Roy chuckled from the back row.

"Very well." Miss Cates sighed and then began doling out our assignments, youngest students first.

Meanwhile, Florence marched down the middle aisle of desks, pausing to elbow Roy in the ribs. He grunted, and the girls next to him giggled. When Miss Cates struck her desk with a ruler, we all snapped back to attention. I'd just put the finishing touches on my writing exercise when Florence returned, and I wondered what had taken her so long. Perhaps Granny's muffins hadn't settled well with her after all, and I had to admit the thought of her in such a nasty predicament made me smile to myself.

Once Miss Cates dismissed the class for the day, she called me up to the front of the room. While I gathered my books, I felt some of the other students watching me, probably wondering if she was going to lecture me. I hadn't broken one of Miss Cates's rules, at least not that I was aware of. Unless maybe she'd decided that handing out baked goods on the school yard wasn't allowed and was going to give me fair warning, which wouldn't really matter because I highly doubted Granny would send me to school with a basketful of muffins ever again. Still, I had to admit I had a few butterflies in my belly as I wove through the desks toward the teacher.

Miss Cates clasped her fingers together and propped them on her desk. "You were right, Red. Your grandmother's muffins are *delicious*. How is she at baking cakes?"

"Only the best in the land," I said. "The king himself would fill his royal dessert table with her cakes if he were ever fortunate enough to try a bite."

"That is quite impressive." She nodded thoughtfully. "Please tell your grandmother that I'd like to have her bake my wedding cake. I'll be in touch with her shortly."

I let out a little squeal and covered my mouth. "Yes, Miss Cates. Thank you. Thank you very much."

"You're welcome, Red." She smiled at me as I took off for the door. The promise of a wedding cake order put a spring in my step. With any more luck, I hoped to find my basket empty and everybody running home to plead with their parents to buy Granny's baked goods. Granny would have more orders coming in than she could fill!

The basket wasn't empty, though. It was full.

Full of *manure*.

For a moment or two, I could do nothing but stare at the horrid brownish-green pile while anger boiled under my skin. Finally, I snapped the lid of the basket shut and dropped it to the ground, but the mucky odor and a swarm of flies lingered.

Clenching my jaw, I scanned the school yard for Violet and her friends. It seemed they'd cleared out, along with most of the others. They all had to help their families get ready for market and other such things. Tasks much more important and pleasant than washing a cow pie out of a basket. Stupid me to have assumed Florence actually needed to use the loo. As if giving Granny a forged muffin order wasn't enough! I was so consumed by rage I didn't even notice Peter until he was right beside me.

"Ready, Red?" he asked. He wrinkled his nose and peered at the bottom of one boot and then the other. "Do you smell something?"

"No," I lied.

He tossed a rusty horsehoe into the air, but I could tell he was trying sneak a sniff in my direction. A couple of boys poked their heads around the corner, obviously waiting for him to come back to the game they'd been playing behind the schoolhouse. "Hold your noses," he called back to them. "I mean, horses. Hold your *horses*." To me he said, "Let me just wrap up this game and then I'm all yours."

All yours, he says. Apart from dancing at the Forget-Me-Not ball with evil Violet. Suddenly, my bodice felt two sizes too tight. "Thank you, but I'd rather walk home by myself today."

Peter raised his left brow. "If you're in a hurry, those rogues can get on just fine without me. It's not a big deal, Red. These matches go on forever, and they always end the same way." He threw the bag at me and I caught it with ease. "Unless you're playing, in which case I sometimes lose."

"No, really. Run along and give those boys a slice of humble pie. I'll see you tomorrow, Peter." I chucked the bag well over his head, but he jumped and managed to catch it anyhow.

I could feel his handsome dark eyes on me as I grabbed my stinking basket and headed for the stream. The ferns and trees became nothing but blurs of green as I passed them, wondering how in the land I'd be able to buy new chickens at market without any money. The bloody, nightmarish scene that had greeted me in the coop that morning flashed before my eyes, and I blinked back the tears. Crouching, I let the chilly springtime water rush into my basket, the stench of manure fitting for the anger that filled my soul.

I hated Violet for tricking Granny into making so many muffins—and worse, for getting Granny's hopes up. I hated Violet most of all for having dug her claws into Peter. Though I tried to stop them, the tears started dripping down my face and into the water. The last traces of Florence's nasty surprise flowed downstream, and while I checked to make sure the basket was clean, I heard footsteps. I turned to see Peter emerging from the trees.

"*Hallo*, Red," he greeted me.

"What are you doing here? I told you to run along and play your game," I said, dabbing my cheeks and nose on my sleeve before standing upright. Usually, I yearned for Peter's company, but not now. Not when I'd been crying.

"I know. I guess I'm not very good at following directions." He shrugged. "But do you want to know something I'm quite good at?"

"I have a feeling you're going to tell me, whether I care to know, or not," I grumbled.

He chuckled. "You know me well, Red. And I know *you*. Something is bothering you, and I'm not letting you go home until you tell me what it is." He spread his legs into a wide stance and blocked my way.

I crossed my arms over my chest and tried not to smile. "It bothers me that you're so smug you think I'm going to spill my heart out to the likes of you," I deadpanned. Deep down, I loved that he'd noticed something wasn't right with me. Still, how could I tell him the truth without sounding jealous? I had no right to feel that way—Peter and I were only friends. "Besides, if I wanted to outrun you, Peter, that's precisely what I'd do."

He chuckled again. "I suppose you have me on that one. Still, I really think you should tell me what's troubling you. You can start by explaining why you're washing your basket out in the stream. I've heard some buzz about the king's new market rules. Is having a sparkling clean food carrier part of this new decree?"

"I wish." I sat on a log, and Peter nestled in beside me. "Instead of the usual apple pie, there was a cow pie in it."

Smirking, he swiped his hair off his forehead. Though I'd been angry only moments ago, now that I thought about it, it was a teensy bit funny. Then his mouth dipped into a frown. "Are you serious?"

I nodded. "I'm afraid so."

"Who would do such a thing? Oh, wait. Let me guess. Violet."

"Well, I think Florence actually did the dirty work, but I have a strong suspicion Violet was the villainous puppeteer."

"I wouldn't put it past her."

Now I was even more confused. It would be one thing if Violet had pulled the wool over his eyes, but if he knew full well how vile she truly was, why would he choose her, of all the girls in all the land?

"But she said you promised her the first dance at the ball," I said. Although the subject probably sounded out of the blue, at least it was finally out there—the thing that was truly bothering me all this time. I didn't know what I expected him to say, but I hoped he'd tell me it was a load of codswallop.

"It's the truth." Peter pinched the bridge of his nose. It looked as though he wanted to say something more. He didn't. And really, what else could he say?

Crestfallen, I turned away from him and pretended to be preoccupied with tapping the excess water out of my basket. "Well, I'm sure the two of you will have a delightful time," I said way too brightly.

Nine

November, three and a half years ago

It had snowed the night of my thirteenth birthday, but my new riding hood kept me dry and cozy while I trekked to school the next morning. The freshly fallen snow was already full of little paw and tail prints; woodland creatures bustled, collecting food and frolicking. I loved how the snowflakes waltzed all around me. Some landed on my nose and on the dark brown waves of hair that had spilled out of my hood.

The flakes that fell on my cape kept their beautiful crystalline shapes for the mere blink of an eye before melting without a trace, their secret visit safe with me.

As soon as I stepped into the school yard, Priscilla

Hanks ran over to me and said, "What a lovely cloak! Is it new?" Priscilla was fifteen and recently betrothed, though she was only two years older than me. She'd kept her romance secret for a couple of months, but we'd started to suspect she and the shoemaker were courting when she showed up wearing a new pair of shoes one week and another new pair the next.

I wanted to be happy for her, but I knew that any day now, she'd stop coming to school altogether, and I'd miss her. They'd still live nearby, just above the shoemaker's shop, and she said I could call on her any time I pleased. Still, I felt sorry for her. Once she married and started a family, chances were slim that she'd ever leave this little village. But perhaps Main Street was as far as her dreams took her.

"Thank you, Priscilla." Delighted, I restrained from twirling and instead swished the sides of the cape a little. By now, several of my classmates had gathered to take a gander at my gift. I knew everyone would notice it; it wasn't very often I had something new, and though most of the girls wore cloaks to keep warm, none I'd seen were half as handsome as mine. I felt beautiful in it, and I liked that feeling. "My granny had it made especially for me, for my birthday," I told them.

Violet joined the ring, and her dark eyes looked me up and down. "Wait, did you just say that your grandmother had this cloak made for you? But . . . it's *red*," she said, stating the obvious.

Priscilla said quietly, "I like it very much."

Violet ignored her and grabbed a small portion of the elegant brocade fabric in her fingers. "You know what they say about a lady in red, don't you?"

I blinked twice, trying to keep my cheeks from heating up. I'd enjoyed the attention Priscilla and the others paid to me, but Violet always had something up her sleeve. I wasn't sure what she was getting at. "Yes, of course," I said. "Red repels wolves, so wearing red clothing protects you from wolves." I blew a strand of hair out of my eyes and muttered, "I'm not stupid."

Violet's grin slowly widened, and she said, "Indeed, you're not," in a tone that made me feel anything but smart. "You know what, Priscilla? I like it very much, too." She let loose the fabric she'd been holding and smoothed it back into place. Next she took several steps back, almost knocking over one of the youngest girls. "And red suits her, don't you agree?"

"I couldn't agree more," Priscilla said.

Violet crossed her arms over her chest and arched an eyebrow. "Good. So it's settled. From now on, her nickname is Red." As Violet joined her friends Beatrice and Florence, who'd been waiting on the steps, news of my new nickname spread rampantly through the school yard.

Everyone seemed to like my nickname, and I did, too; but a question nagged at me while I tried to finish my arithmetic problems later that day. I whispered in Priscilla's ear, "What was Violet talking about when she called me 'a lady in red'?"

Priscilla shrugged. "I don't know, but I wouldn't worry about it. She's green with envy. Just look how much finer your cloak is than her plain beige one. Besides, I remember when her sister, Nicola, wore that very cloak she's wearing. Violet probably wishes she had a new one, like you. Remember all those spiteful things she said about me, that the only reason Timothy wants to marry me is because I'm tall, and he doesn't want any son of his to be as short as he?"

I nodded, embarrassed on Priscilla's behalf. It made her sound like nothing better than a hound that's chosen to breed because it's a good hunter. "I'm sure it's not true, Priscilla. You have many good qualities. Being tall just happens to be one of them."

"That's kind of you to say. Thank you." She briefly smiled before continuing. "At first I was furious at Violet for saying such things. Then I realized that she was merely jealous. Saying such a thing was her petty little way of getting back at me for having such nice new shoes. I could have said or done something back to her, but I figure that the best vengeance is forever being the bigger person. Or, in this case, marrying the man Nicola had been batting her eyes at for a good six months!" We laughed, and my mood instantly lifted.

However, it wasn't long before I figured out what Violet meant by "lady in red."

Once school let out, Peter invited me to join him and his buddies to go sledding down the big hill behind the church. After we built jumps with mounds of snow, Peter handed me his sled, saying, "Ladies first." To be candid, the jumps were so high, and the hill so steep . . . I was frightened. I wanted someone else to go before me. Even then, I wasn't sure if I could muster the courage to go. "Come on, I'll be right behind you. It'll be a whale of a time. You'll see!"

"I think you just want me to go first because you're chicken," I said tauntingly. I knew Peter would never back down from a challenge. The first group raced down the hill, hooting and hollering, leaving Tucker Williamson and me alone at the top.

Tucker Williamson was thirteen, like me. He was scrawny, spotty-skinned, and mean as a badger. Plus, he always had whitish powder in his hair—probably because he was the miller's son. No one really liked him much, but Peter felt sorry for him and oftentimes asked him along on our after-school adventures. I usually just ignored Tucker, but that was difficult to do when it was just the two of us. So I smiled at him and hoped the others would be back soon.

His eyes gleamed in a way I'd never seen. It was like he saw me as a nice venison tenderloin one second, and a roach he wanted to trample with his boot—or squish with his bare hand—the very next. My stomach churned, and I drew my cloak tightly over my shoulders. *What's taking Peter and the others so long?* "Looks like they're having fun," I said as airily as I could. "I can't wait to go. How about you?"

Tucker slid his hand down the side of my cloak. Then he grabbed the other side of it and pulled me up against him.

"What are you doing?" I tried to push him away. The next thing I knew, Tucker Williamson's hideous face was in my face, and his lips were coming horrifyingly close to mine. I smelled his wretched breath and got a close-up view of his snaggletooth. Screaming, I twisted and squirmed, but he had a death grip on my cloak. I forged just enough slack to unfasten my cloak and shove him off of me. Next I kneed him as hard as I could, right in the crotch. He doubled over, groaning, as I hopped out of his reach, lost my balance, and tumbled to the soft, snowy ground.

"Why did you do that?" Tucker coughed. "I thought that's what you wanted. That's what she said you wanted—why you wear that red riding hood." Gone was the look of a predator, and in its place, utter bafflement. I, too, was confused.

"Who in the land would say I wanted that?" I asked breathlessly. But the instant the question left my mouth, I knew.

Thankfully, Peter and the boys had heard my cries and were trudging up the hill as quickly as possible over knee-deep drifts. Peter, pulling his sled behind him, would be to the top of the hill in mere seconds.

"What the dickens is going on here?" Peter demanded,

helping me up. "Tucker, you bastard, what did you do to her?" Peter took him by the collar of his coat and shook him. Fury blazed in Peter's eyes, and he looked fit to be tied.

"N-n-nothing," Tucker said, shrinking into his coat like a turtle. "I didn't do anything to her, honest."

"Then why did she scream? Why was she down in the snow?" Now that the other three boys were there, Peter loosened his hold on Tucker and turned to me. He stared at me with an intensity I'd never seen in him. "Did he hurt you?"

Careful not to have eye contact with Tucker, I refastened and brushed the white powder off my cloak. "No. He didn't hurt me," I admitted.

Peter stepped closer to me and whispered in my ear, "Did he touch you?" He opened and closed his fist as he awaited my answer.

I shook my head no. "He touched my cloak, that's all."

"I was only admiring it," Tucker said.

"Well, next time, admire it from afar. Maybe this will

help you remember," Peter said, before hitting him hard, square in the jaw. Tucker groaned and rubbed the side of his face.

The whole thing gave me a rush of emotions from fear to pity to awe. The other boys turned their backs on Tucker, and Peter offered to take me home. But if I went home right then, I'd have to part ways with Peter too soon.

"Not until I've had my turn," I said, taking his sled. As I raced down the hill, my hood blew off, and my hair and cloak danced freely in the wind. I laughed as I careened over the snow, going faster and faster until, finally, the slope flattened out and brought me to a gentle halt. I rolled onto my back and found the evening star. It was all alone, but I knew that in no time, the sky would be sparkling with stars.

It was hard to make sense of my emotions, but even after Violet's snide comments and Tucker's unwelcome advance, I still felt cozy, safe, and beautiful in my new red cloak. The night before, on my thirteenth birthday,

I'd promised my granny I'd wear it—and, in a way, I'd extended that promise to my mother. And then, once I'd had my share of sledding and Peter had insisted we head home, he said, "You probably don't care, but I think your new cloak is rather . . . becoming." He kicked a clump of snow on the side of the road.

"Thank you, Peter," I said. In my heart, those three little words covered much more than the compliment he'd paid my cloak. I was thanking him for having stuck up for me and for being my friend, then and always.

"You're welcome, Red." My new nickname sounded so wonderful on Peter's lips.

Ten

Folks came from near and far to sell their goods,
perform, and have first pickings at the village market.
Granny was aiming to sell more pies and cookies than
ever before, so we'd left the cottage as soon as I'd gotten
home from school, hoping to secure a desirable spot in
the center.

As we trudged along with our overstuffed baskets,
Granny said, "I just don't understand." Though I sweated
beneath my cloak, she'd draped an extra shawl over her
shoulders and looked cool as a cucumber. "You say your
schoolmarm didn't have enough money for the muffins.
And yet, she has the audacity to ask me to bake her wedding cake. What kind of flapdoodle is that?"

I could have told Granny what had really happened, but I chose not to. I had a terrible feeling she'd march right up to Violet and her whole clan and force them to pay up—or do something even more drastic if she was in a particularly foul mood. Starting a feud between us and the Roberts family would not end well, that much I knew.

On the contrary, Granny would never confront Miss Cates about the muffins. My grandmother might not be the most devout woman in the village, and she was quick to make jokes behind the vicar's back, but she knew better than to vex the betrothed of a man of God.

"Maybe you could ask Miss Cates for payment up front this time," I suggested, but Granny shook her head emphatically and said, "No, no, that's not how I do it."

"So make her the wedding cake," I suggested, "and I have a very good feeling she will have more than enough money to pay. Besides, think of all the people who will see and taste your beautiful creation. I have no doubt that a cake for Vicar Clemmons and his bride will earn you more business than you will know what to do with."

"Yes, you might have a point there . . ." Granny said and then fell silent in thought as we plodded along. We'd almost made it to market when she stopped to set down her basket and catch her breath. "Go ahead without me, Red. Set up shop on the shady side. I'll be right behind you."

"Are you sure, Granny?"

She smacked the back of my head. "Of course I'm sure. Otherwise, I wouldn't have said a word about it. Here's a list of ingredients I need. Bargain and barter with the sellers like I've taught you." She dropped a slip of parchment and some coins into my hand. "Now, git!"

"Only if you let me carry this for you." Before she had the chance to refuse, I picked up her basket and walked away.

When I finally arrived at market, my hands ached and throbbed with the threat of blisters. I wanted nothing more than to stake claim on a spot and relax while the other vendors fought for space. A puppeteer troop in a ramshackle carriage, an old gypsy couple in a colorfully patched tent, a portly potter, and a few farmers had already arrived. Soon the space would be crammed with artisans, entertainers, and merchants of every sort imaginable.

Distracted by the sounds and views, I didn't even notice the man blocking my path until it was too late. I came to such an abrupt stop I dropped the baskets. The man wore a ridiculous three-pointed hat with a feather and had the gall to neither step away nor apologize.

"I didn't see you there," I said, bending to collect the coins and buns that had rolled out onto the cobblestones.

A black boot slammed down on the coins. "Where are you off to, missy?" the man asked.

"I'm setting up my baked goods for market," I replied, even more annoyed at the stupidity of his question than the fact that he'd almost stepped on my hand. "So if you'll kindly move your foot, I'll gather my things and be on with it."

He knelt beside me and picked up the money. With his free hand, he stroked his long black beard. "A prime spot in the market will cost you all of this. A spot over yonder, by the farmers, will cost you half, and if you dare set up in the alley," he said, nudging his head in the direction of the gypsies, "this much." He dropped about a fourth of the coins into my hand.

"You must be jesting," I said. I tried to laugh, but it got stuck in my throat. This stranger had an air about him, and it smelled of rotten eggs. "Who do you think you are? My grandmother and I have been coming to market for years, and not once have we been required to pay."

Folks were arriving from all directions with their goods to sell. At the forefront was Amos Slade and his ever-loyal hound dog. As usual, the lanky old hunter had brought a cart full of venison and an assortment of pelts to market.

The hound growled at the man in the funny hat—or perhaps he was growling at me—bringing me back to the present. Amos had stopped right beside us and said to the man, "What's goin' on here? Leave the Lucas girl alone."

The man stood and straightened his hat. "So you're the granddaughter of Widow Lucas?" he asked me.

"Perhaps. And who are you?" I retorted.

"My name is Hershel Worthington, and on behalf of the king, I'm to collect fees for market vendors, beginning today. See here?" He dug a scroll out of his satchel, unrolled it, and held it up as if it were a fine painting. From my vantage point, all I could tell was that it was written in fancy script. As Amos read it, his bushy mustache fanned out, and he snorted like an angry bull.

Mr. Worthington held the scroll higher, and a crowd began gathering around us. "Quite unfortunate that some villagers—this young lady's grandmother, for instance—" he said, holding his other hand over my head, "are overdue on their taxes."

Surely Mr. Worthington had Granny mixed up with somebody else. "What are you talking about?" I asked.

"It's quite simple. When I went to your house to collect taxes, she did not pay. Now, where was I? Oh, yes." He cleared his throat. "This leaves His Royal Highness no choice but to enforce decrees such as this. Our benevolent ruler apologizes for the inconvenience, and sends from the royal castle his best wishes for a prosperous season."

As Amos reached in his pocket and paid the tax man, he let out a stream of curses almost equal to Granny's best. In turn, several other villagers surrendered their money. Sidling up to me, Mr. Worthington asked, "And what option have you decided upon, Miss Lucas?"

"Give me back the money, Mr. Worthington," I said between clenched teeth. "All of it. I will not be buying a vendor spot today."

His squinty, bloodshot eyes dipped from my face to my neck and rested on my heaving chest. A hundred scorching baths with every last bar of Granny's soap wouldn't wash away the feeling of disgust I felt at that moment. "As you wish," he said, and dropped the coins one by one into my palm.

Holding my head as high as possible, I turned my back to him and began collecting the baskets. It would've been great if I could have stormed off for effect. However, my knees trembled, and the baskets were so heavy and bulky I probably looked like a hobbled mule in a red blanket as I clomped away from him and down a side street.

As folks wandered by on their way to market, I tried to erase my mind of the tax man and how he'd publicly humiliated Granny and me. I asked the villagers if they'd like to buy a cinnamon roll or a pie, and little by little, the baskets emptied, and I collected their meager payments. Every so often, I exchanged a half-dozen date cookies for spices or something else on Granny's shopping list. Nevertheless, my heart sunk with the knowledge that even without having paid the tax man his outrageous market fee, and even if I eventually sold every last crumb of Granny's baked goods, I wouldn't have enough money to replace our chickens. And now Mr. Worthington seemed to believe Granny owed him taxes.

An old farmer wheeled his cart around the bend, and as he passed the tavern, a big green apple rolled off the back. I tried to get his attention, but he was too busy pleading with his pouting wife to notice. I shrugged and added it to my basket. One apple off of Granny's shopping list left us twenty-three shy.

Other than a pair of pigeons that appeared to be lost, I was basically alone on my little village corner. By then, Granny should have arrived, and I knew I should check on her. Plus I wanted to ask her about the taxes. So I stacked the remaining baked goods into a single basket, stashed the empty one under some stairs, and began tracking her down.

The market was in full swing. The sounds of voices shouting and singing and the music of tambourines, horns, drums, flutes, and accordions blared. Shading my eyes with my hand, I wove in and out of the crowd looking for Granny and pausing every so often to peddle a pie. Thankfully, the last one, an apple pie, found a new home. Granny would be pleased.

My grandmother had lived in the village her whole life, so even if someone hadn't met her in person, almost everybody at least knew of her. "Excuse me, have you by chance seen my grandmother, the Widow Lucas, today?" I asked the tall woman hawking satchels and belts. Rather, *trying* to, as no one seemed interested in her wares.

The infant tucked into the woman's hip-sling cried, and she muttered, "Hush, now," to him before turning in my direction. My heart warmed as I recognized the young mother's eyes. "I'm sorry, what did you say?" Priscilla asked.

Behind her, a boy and a girl who looked to be about two years old played with a wooden whirligig. A black-and-white mutt with a sweet face sat at the twins' feet; yet for some strange reason, as soon as he sniffed me, he darted behind his mistress's banner, tail tucked between his legs.

"Red!"

My old schoolmate had plumped up, and lines had settled under her eyes. Yet the blond tresses that poured out of her shawl gleamed brilliantly in the sunshine, and her cheeks were a pretty shade of pink.

"Priscilla! It's been ages." When Priscilla first married the shoemaker, three years ago, they had ordered Granny's baked goods almost every week. In addition, Granny used to bring me into the shoemaker's shop more often back then, since my feet were still growing.

Look at her now: a mother with a trio of spirited carrottopped children. And though I oftentimes found it sad that Priscilla had settled for an unadventurous life as the wife of the pallid shoemaker, she actually looked happy.

"It looks like someone drank her mead," I teased, speaking of the local tradition where newlyweds become fertile after downing the honey liquor for a month. "I want to hug you, but I'm afraid I might crush that adorable baby of yours," I said. "He is rather tiny." It was hard to believe such a little peanut would someday grow into a full-sized man. Or, if he took after his father, a half-sized man.

Priscilla laughed and gave me a gentle side hug anyhow. The infant stopped fussing and gaped at me with round, slate blue eyes and dewy lips in the shape of an "o." "Look at that, my little Ezekiel is quite fond of you." I never knew I could soothe a baby, and I felt like I'd discovered a new magical power. "I'm glad to see you still wear your beautiful red riding hood. What kind of mischief have you been into, Red? Tell me everything— every last detail." She grabbed my hand and gave it a squeeze.

"Hallo?" An elderly man tapped his cane on the ground to get Priscilla's attention. "I say, *hallo.* How much for that belt there, with the pouch?"

"I apologize, Red," she whispered. "I do want to catch up, but I have to sell twice as much as last week to balance the new market fee. And all of this in the shadow of the tax collection."

"I understand," I said, smiling. "Maybe I can come by again, a bit later on."

"Yes, please do. And best of luck finding your grandmother." She released my hand and turned her attention to her customer. I was glad to see that several other folks were wandering over to peruse her wares. When I passed some crates of clucking chickens, I paused to hear how much the farmer was selling them for. There was almost enough in my satchel, but I still needed to buy or trade for the items on Granny's list.

I figured I might as well wrap up the shopping as I searched for Granny. I tapped my toes while a woman dug deep into the bushels and scrupulously examined each and every piece of fruit before placing it in her bag. "This isn't enough," the ruddy-faced farmer said after counting the coins she'd paid him. He told her how much more she owed.

"My, oh, my," she said, crossing her arms over her ample bosom. "Unless your pears are enchanted, that price is outlandish and I refuse to pay it." She made a big production of taking the fruit out of her bag and tossing it back on his cart.

"Suit yourself, you wretched old miser," he huffed. "Now, shoo. I don't need your sort scaring off all my *sensible* customers." As soon as the farmer turned to me and asked, "What can I do for you, young lady?" a mob-like commotion exploded from outside the town hall. The people around me dropped what they were in the midst of doing and migrated toward the hubbub, including the farmer. The pears the woman had returned started rolling, taking some apples with them. I reached over to stop the fruit-fall, and in doing so, something came over me.

I'd never been a thief, and never thought I'd be tempted to steal, even a little bit. But if I could get the ingredients on the list and keep the money in my satchel, we would be able to buy the chickens we so sorely needed. "I'll pay you back someday," I whispered as I stealthily slid pears, apples, and nuts beneath my cloak and then slipped them into my basket.

My heart thudding, I glanced this way and that. Although I felt a thousand disapproving eyes on me, it must have been only my conscience playing tricks. No one seemed to be paying me any mind. I sidestepped to the next cart—this one the miller's. A sack of flour was a bit more of a challenge to sneak from my cloak into the basket, especially without smashing the remaining cookies and rolls, but I inexplicably managed. With sweaty, shaky hands, I clutched my basket, which grew rapidly heavier with each pilfered item. Yet an oddly wonderful feeling flowed through my veins. Could it be that I was actually good at stealing?

The candles I needed beckoned to me from the next booth, but as I trundled them into my basket, I felt the pang of a sharp object in my knee. I thought for sure I'd been caught red-handed, but luckily, it was only Seamstress Evans's little pirate boy.

"Gimme a cookie."

"You'd better be careful," I said, moving the toy sword off my knee. "If you chop off my leg, I'll be stuck hobbling around on a wooden peg. I don't know about you, but I'd hate to be accused of being a pirate."

Snarling, the boy pointed the sword up at my face.

"Or you could put an eye out," I continued. "And who wants to wear a black patch over their eye? Well, it looks as if you do, but not me."

He lowered his wooden weapon to the ground, tracing the cobblestones with its tip. "Come on, I want a cookie. Yours are the best in the land."

"If I give you a treat, will you leave me in peace?" I asked, and he nodded excitedly. I opened the lid of my basket just a hair. The boy watched with a curious expression on his freckled mug as I blindly felt around. It was as if the stolen flour, fruit, and candles were playing a game with me, one in which the object was to never let me get hold of a cookie. Finally, I found one and handed it to him with a smile. "Ah, oatmeal raisin. My personal favorite. You're very lucky I even have one left."

He scrunched his snotty little nose. "Do you have a sugar cookie?"

"Sorry, I'm all out."

"Don't you have any that aren't broken, then? Come on, I'm sure you do."

I glanced up to see Tucker Williamson straightening the burlap sacks on his father's cart. With muscular arms and towering over six feet tall, Tucker had grown into a giant compared to the boy I'd kneed in the groin on the snow-covered hill behind the church. That was the day Peter and the other boys stopped feeling sorry for him and stopped including him in their fun and games. Ever after, Tucker had become something of a lone wolf, working for his family and showing up at school only rarely.

"My pa said he was about to help you," Tucker said, "but now he's caught up in some kind of political debate over yonder. He told me to come and get you your flour."

"Oh. Um, thanks, but I don't need any today. I'm just passing through, searching for my grandmother. She's probably working out some kind of deal, knowing her. Quite the savvy businesswoman, you know." I tittered nervously.

"She doesn't need any flour because she already has a sack in her basket," said the glib pirate boy before he scurried off with the oatmeal cookie.

Tucker's eyebrows arched as he peered down at me. "Have you?"

My whole face blazed. I took a step back, almost tripping. "That little scallywag has an active imagination, all right," I said with a chuckle. "Did you know he truly believes he's a pirate?" I chuckled again, as if my nervousness was bubbling out of me. I might as well have had a sign hung around my neck proclaiming I AM A THIEF! for all to read.

"Come on, Red. Let's see what's in the basket." Tucker's hand moved in for the handle. I silently urged my legs to run, but they wouldn't budge. If I merely stood before him, it was only a matter of seconds before he'd find the evidence he needed to expose me. Instead of helping Granny and me get back on solid footing, we'd slip further into debt and dishonor. *I can't let that happen. I won't!*

I was completely parched, yet managed to utter, "Something sweet, just for you." As my foreign-sounding words hung in the air, I set the basket on the ground and took a deep breath. I closed the space between us, reaching up for his massive shoulders with both of my arms.

Pulling him in, I rose onto my tiptoes and closed my eyes. *Now!* In a tangle of hands, necks, chins, and finally, lips, I kissed him.

I kissed Tucker Williamson.

What have I done?

Eleven

I wrenched myself away from Tucker and touched my lips, expecting them to smack of bitterness or sting as if I'd rubbed poison oak on them—or, even worse, be covered with warts. Apart from the uneasiness churning in my belly, it appeared I had indeed survived, even if by my last shred of luck.

I was too mortified to make eye contact, but I felt him staring at me. "What . . . ? Why . . . ?" he stammered.

"Sorry, Tucker, but I . . . I have to go." I turned on my heels and smoothed the wrinkles out of my cloak. "I need to find my grandmother."

As I bolted toward the town hall, I heard him call after me, "Red, wait!"

Shaking my head, I shouldered my way through the throng. One by one, young and old, the villagers' eyes hardened with judgments as they looked at me. It felt as if my boots were laden with rocks, each step more grueling than the last. I touched the gold cross on my chest, and next my lips. *They know what I've done.* If I hadn't had to collect Granny first, I would have fled the market and gone straight home. *Everybody knows.*

Once I was near enough to the soapbox to see and hear who was stirring up such a hullabaloo, I understood why the people really pitied me. As horrible as kissing Tucker Williamson had been—especially had everybody known about it—I gladly would have done it again, if only I could have stopped Granny from making a fool of herself. From making a fool of the both of us.

"We've all lost chickens, lambs, and cows," Granny shouted as people stared at her, some of them laughing, some scowling. "The wolves' hunger grows, and it's only a matter of time before they hunt for human blood. They have before, and mark my words, they will again.

Whenever the moon is full, we must not wander around the village or traipse in the woods. We must stay in our homes. We cannot allow our young people to have parties and bonfires around Wolfstime." She gasped for air, and though I stood five rows back, I saw beads of sweat on her brow. I felt dampness on my brow, as well. "This is why the Forget-Me-Not ball cannot be held on its traditional night this year." She pointed at the poster that Violet and her friends had made last week at school and hung in the window of the town hall. "The moon will be full. The wolves will hunt. We cannot lose our young people to the beasts!"

The crowd roared, the vast majority of its members sniggering or elbowing one another. I shut my eyes, wishing I could magically disappear. When I opened my eyes again, two tomatoes were flying straight for my head; I ducked just in time to miss being pelted. I swung around and glared at the culprits: a group of children—including the pirate boy and one of Peter's little brothers—perched on a ladder. A head of cabbage hit Granny right in the bosom, making the people point and snigger even more. And if that weren't enough of a nightmare, I caught a whiff of honeysuckle. Before I could count to three, Violet, Beatrice, and Florence materialized beside me.

"Your dear grandmother is off her rickety ole rocker if she honestly believes she can sabotage our ball," Florence said, raking her fingers through her reddish locks. Violet and Beatrice wore matching sneers.

Granny eased her way off the soapbox, and the villagers cheered to have her gone. Taking my arm, Violet led me away from her friends. "Your granny isn't the only one with crazy thoughts. Silly me, I was under the impression you fancied Peter. Lo and behold, it's Tucker you are pining for. It's not often I misread people so badly."

I hadn't realized my jaw had gone slack until I tried to respond—and even then, I felt as if the air had been knocked out of my lungs. "I don't like Tucker. I can barely even stomach him."

Little by little, Violet raised her eyebrows. "I see. So if you can't stand Tucker, why did you *kiss* him?"

I coughed, and when my voice came out, it croaked like a frog. "What? You saw that?" How could I explain that I'd only kissed him in desperation, to distract him from searching my basket?

"I was afraid that snaggletooth of his would snag your lip," she said, clapping me on the back and laughing. "Don't worry, Red. I wouldn't dream of telling anyone. It will be our little secret. Yours, mine, and Tucker Williamson's." I wanted to believe her, but the way her eyes gleamed told me that if it was indeed a secret now, it wouldn't be for long.

A breeze stirs the air, and on it drifts the voice of my dreams. "Only when you refuse to be a victim of fear will you know your true power."

The wind picks up, freeing my hair of its braids, lifting my cloak like wings. Raising my eyes skyward, I see the dark gray clouds part, revealing the full moon in all of its silvery-white brilliance.

"I don't know what you mean." It's my voice saying this, yet I am not speaking out loud. "Please, tell me."

I listen for a response; instead, I hear angry shouts. And they're getting louder, nearer. Too close.

They're coming for me.

Tuesday, May 15

"Wake up, sleepyhead! Didn't you hear the rooster?" After yanking the pillow out from under my head, Granny unlocked and opened my window. I squeezed my eyes shut, but still I heard her breathing in the morning air, making a horrible wheezing sound. "I thought you'd like hearing the rooster crow. It means the wolves stayed out of our chicken coop last night. Sure is nice having chickens again. I'm not sure how you did it, but—"

"I bartered and bargained, just like you taught me." I groaned and burrowed deep into the covers. "Now, please go away."

"Why so grumpy, child? Did you not get enough winks last night?"

My Wolfstime dream had been particularly disturbing. The darkness had been so intense; it clung to my skin and seeped into my mouth and eyes.

Now that I was awake, I feared that another horrible nightmare awaited me. This one had long ebony curls, shiny boots, and a slippery grip on my secret.

"I think I'm coming down with something," I said, and though I knew it wasn't a traditional ailment, I truly did feel sick to my stomach. "I shouldn't go to school."

I heard Granny stomp back to my bedside. She flipped the blankets off me and pressed her hand to my forehead. A moment later, she exclaimed, "Rubbish! You're as fit as a fiddle. You're going to school, and you're going to learn. It's bad enough that school's held only three times a week nowadays. I won't have people say I'm raising the village idiot. Now, get up and get going. Your porridge is getting cold."

"Well, perhaps I should skip school today and try to sell some extra baked goods," I said, hoisting myself up onto my elbows. "While I was at market, a dreadful man called Hershel Worthington told me that you didn't pay your taxes when he came by to collect. Is that true?"

The furrows in Granny's forehead deepened. "Now why in the land would he say that to you?"

"He told a whole crowd of folks who were setting up at market."

Slit-eyed, she stared out my window. I couldn't read if she was angry or mortified—maybe both.

"So, is it true, Granny?" I repeated.

She blinked and adjusted her glasses on her nose. "He offered me an extension. I gave him a two-day-old pie—told him I'd taken it out of the oven that morning, but he's just a fool so he didn't know the difference—and he said he'd come back on Thursday for the money."

"You have the money, right?"

"We haven't been working this hard for nothing. Everything will work out just fine. Always does. Nothing to worry about. Not that it's any of your business, anyhow. Going to school is your business, you hear me? So get up out of this bed right now. Your breakfast is probably cold by now."

Cold porridge didn't matter to me, because after I

dressed and braided my hair, my stomach was still not faring well enough to eat. If anything, it felt worse.

As soon as I set foot in the school yard, a brigade of little boys made squeaky kissing noises from up in the climbing tree. One went so far as to face the tree, wrap his arms around himself, and rub his hands up and down his back, pretending to be getting frisky with someone. Whether they'd heard about me kissing Tucker Williamson, or they were just teasing me the way they did all the girls, I couldn't be certain. I figured that bypassing the tree—even if it meant cutting too close to the girls skipping rope—wouldn't hurt.

Violet, Florence, and Beatrice sat on the front steps, talking and laughing as usual. The pair of younger girls next to them stopped their game of ringers. One whispered in the other's ear, and both pairs of eyes were glued on me.

Taking a deep breath, I reached for my golden cross

and held it between my thumb and finger. Violet smiled at me as I approached. It wasn't a friendly smile—yet it wasn't evil, either. It was more of a secretive smile. Then she waved. Not only the marble girls, but Florence and Beatrice looked up at me, so I reluctantly waggled my fingers.

Then I heard someone clear his throat and peered over my shoulder. Tucker Williamson stood behind me wearing a dingy gray shirt and a smug expression. I clenched my jaw at the realization that Violet's greeting had actually been for Tucker, not me. It took everything I had to keep my head held high as I stepped out of his path.

He breezed past me and brazenly sidled up to the girls on the steps. It had been a long time since the big, spotty-faced boy had come to school. And when he did, he never sat with anyone, let alone Violet Roberts. Everybody in the school yard seemed as curious and riveted as I was. Even the eldest boys, Peter and his chums, came out from behind the schoolhouse to see what was going on. All I could gather was that Violet was preparing for a puppet show, and Tucker was her latest marionette. I had the sinking feeling that I was about to have my strings pulled, as well.

After a brief moment of banter that appeared pleasant enough, Violet raised her voice and prompted, "What's that, Tucker? You were telling me what happened at market . . ."

Tucker's eyes twitched as though he'd swallowed a fly. "Red kissed me."

My knees buckled, and I wished my riding hood had been enchanted with a vanishing spell rather than a protection-from-wolves one. I knew that seeing or hearing anyone's reaction would be pure agony, especially Peter's—so why I rashly sought him out, I couldn't say. It was as if the darkest shadow had fallen on Peter's handsome face. He looked like a stranger, which crushed my heart. Shaking his head, he walked away, and his buddies followed him back around the schoolhouse.

I wanted to tell him to come back—it wasn't true! I

wanted to tell myself it wasn't. But of course I couldn't, because although Violet was the one exposing it to the whole school, I only had myself to blame for having kissed Tucker in the first place.

"Red, I take it you and Tucker are courting now?" Violet asked, and I clenched my fists.

"No," I said softly.

She tapped her chin and pursed her lips together. "So when you kissed him, it meant nothing?"

"That's right." I swallowed, wishing she'd make her point already, and let me get on with my miserable life.

"It's a good thing your name is Red, rather than Chastity," she said, and the school yard burst into exclamations of shock and amusement. I hazarded a glance at Tucker, whose ruddy face twisted into an odd expression—like he wanted to laugh along with the others, but he feared that at any moment he might throw up. I knew how he felt with the throwing-up part. When our eyes met, a lump formed in my throat. Perhaps what I'd done to him was even crueler than what he'd done on the sledding hill so long ago.

As soon as Miss Cates dismissed us for the day, I tethered my books and hurried to the road without talking to anyone. I couldn't get away from the schoolhouse fast enough, and I was relieved I didn't have to go tomorrow. Against all odds, I hoped the story about me kissing Tucker would die down before Thursday.

I hadn't made it far down the road before Peter caught up with me. "*Hallo*, Red. Mind if I walk you home?" he asked.

"If it makes you happy."

"Of course it makes me happy. That's why I do it." We walked to the swale in silence, and then he jumped in front of me and asked, "Are you all right? You barely looked up from your desk all day."

"I've never been better," I lied. "Listen, about Tucker. I . . ." I had no idea what to say, but I knew better than to pretend nothing had happened.

"I hoped he was lying," Peter said after a moment. "I hoped Violet was blackmailing him or something. But I could tell by the look in your eyes that what he said was true." Peter twisted a dead twig off a tree and broke it in two. "I don't get it, Red. You can do so much better than Tucker Williamson. He's a bastard." He tossed one piece of the twig behind me, and the other he flung to the side of the road.

I felt as if my emotions were being torn in two separate directions, too. My eyes burned, and I feared that at any second I'd start sobbing. But I didn't want to cry in front of Peter. I wouldn't allow myself to be sad. Instead, I focused on my growing anger.

I was cross with everyone: myself for getting into this humiliating and horrible mess in the first place; Granny for leaving me at market with an impossible shopping list; Violet for somehow persuading Tucker to tell the whole school that I'd kissed him; Tucker for giving in to Violet, *and* for suspecting that I'd stolen the flour, *and* for choosing today of all days to come to school; and even the little pirate boy for ratting me out to Tucker. Not even Peter, whom I was usually quite fond of, was safe from my wrath at that moment.

"While we're sharing opinions," I said, sidestepping

Peter and continuing down the road, "I think you can do better than Violet Roberts, as well."

"It's not what it seems," he said.

"Oh, really?" I whirled around and put my hands on my hips. "Then please tell me how it *is*, Peter. What exactly happened between Violet and you on the night of your birthday?"

"Your grandmother came to the bonfire, searching for you. I wanted to go with her to help find you, but she said I'd only slow her down." He took a deep breath and kicked at some pebbles. "Then Violet took me aside and told me she knew which direction you'd taken off in, and she'd tell me for a price."

"Let me guess. The price was dancing with her at the ball?"

"Not at first. In the beginning, she wanted me to dance with her right then and there at the bonfire. I kept trying to get her to tell me where you'd gone, but Gregory kept on fiddling, and she still hadn't held up her side of the bargain. I told her I'd dance with her at the ball if she'd tell me that very minute. It was rash on my part, but I couldn't think of a better plan, and I knew the longer I was stuck dancing with her at the party, the farther you'd have traveled. I know you're afraid of the wolves, Red, and I couldn't bear to think of you wandering around the dark woods without so much as a torch. I wanted to be there for you."

I blinked. "You wanted to protect me?" Suddenly, all the anger that had been building up inside of me started to ebb.

"Of course I did. I *do*." He held out his arms, and I pressed my entire body into his warm embrace. I closed my eyes and rested my head against his shoulder. He smelled like the first rays of sunshine after a spring shower.

"You're my *friend*, Red," he murmured into my hair. "I'd feel horrible if anything bad ever happened to you."

Friends, yes. That's what we are.

I took a step away from him, and then another. I knew I should be happy and grateful to have a friend like Peter.

I should be thrilled that the only reason he'd agreed to dance with Violet at the ball was to find out which direction I'd run—because he wanted to protect me.

Yet, as we hugged on the road that afternoon, I felt something shift deep within my heart. It was blissfully wonderful and excruciatingly painful all at once. I knew with complete certainty that I wanted Peter to be more than my friend.

I was falling in love with him.

Just before twilight, Granny and I darted about the cottage, lost in our own thoughts as we prepared for Wolfstime. When she pulled the portcullis over the fireplace, she grunted as usual, but suddenly, her grunt turned into a shriek. I dropped the cups of cider on the table and ran to her.

Grasping her right arm, she said breathlessly, "I'm all right. I'm all right."

"You are *not* all right, Granny," I said as I helped her onto her favorite spot on the sofa. "You're in agony. And it's getting worse, isn't it?" Now that I thought about it, when I'd come home from school that afternoon, she'd been in her bedroom instead of in the kitchen baking. As I put together other oddities, such as there being only a few baked goods on the kitchen counter, packaged and ready for me to deliver in the morning, and Granny's quietness in general—which I'd admittedly found refreshing, especially since I had so much weighing on my mind—I realized how selfish I'd been not to have noticed earlier. "Does it hurt too much to bake?"

"After tonight, there's only three more nights to go. And then plenty of time to recoup before the next Wolfstime." Her quivering lips formed the slightest of smiles.

As I sopped up the spilled cider and topped off our cups with more, I hoped the smile on my face was more convincing. However, Granny had to make it through four more nights and three more days. It would not be easy. "I wish there was something I could do," I said.

She clicked her tongue. "Don't waste something as precious as a wish on something so silly. I'll survive. Always do. That is, unless I have to bake another damn muffin. I swear, I have no inkling why people are suddenly so cuckoo over my muffins."

"They're delicious, that's why." I was glad to hear that giving out muffin samples was paying off.

"Well, I can't argue with that." We sipped our ciders without speaking for quite a while. Finally, she sighed and said, "You should be getting to bed, child."

I nodded and brought the cups back to the kitchen. I might not have been able to relieve Granny's pain, but perhaps I could bake something in the morning and help her keep on top of her orders.

Twelve

On the ground, small round rocks glow in the moonlight, illuminating my path like thousands of tiny lanterns. I tear off through the forest, running faster than ever before. But somehow, the path leads me in a circle, straight to the torches, swords, pitchforks, and spears.

I'm filled with overwhelming sadness, and I feel tears run down my chin. But when I wipe it, I am shocked and horrified to see that the wetness is not tears, but blood.

Wednesday, May 16

"No!"

I sat straight up, coughing. My heart pounded in my

chest, and sweat coated my skin. As I blinked, the familiar shadows of my bedroom finally came into focus. It was still dark, so it must've been the middle of the night, or perhaps very early in the morning. When I swallowed, I tasted blood.

Granny hurried into my bedroom, shouting, "What is it, child? Are you all right?" By the glow of her candle, I could make out the rag curlers in her gray hair and the look of alarm in her eyes. But I didn't want her to know I was afraid, so I said, "I'm fine, Granny. It was just a silly nightmare. I must have bitten my tongue."

She slid her glasses up the bridge of her nose. After using her candle to enkindle my bedside light, she held it by my face. "Yes, it appears you did. Does it hurt?"

"No, it's *fine*, Granny. Everything is fine," I said, before taking a swig of water to rinse out the salty, coppery taste in my mouth.

She took her handkerchief out of her robe pocket and gently dabbed off the blood from my lips. Next she placed the back of her hand on my forehead. "You feel warm."

"That's because you make me wear this ridiculous tent of a nightgown." Of course, I wasn't going to admit that the real reason I was wearing a gown was in case Peter happened to come by the cottage to check on me again. "I have no choice but to sweat all night long," I said, wriggling out of her reach.

"Perspire," she corrected me, and I scrunched my nose.

"Fine, whatever. Perspire. But I'm perspiring like a pig."

"It's my job to raise you to be proper, and proper young ladies sleep in nightdresses. You should be grateful that yours are so pretty and fit well. Not every girl is as fortunate." Granny folded her handkerchief over and patted it along my hairline. "That must have been some dream," she said. "Do you want to tell me about it?"

"It was just a normal dream, I'm sure—the kind everybody has. Don't worry about it, Granny. Go back to bed. I mean, go back to sofa."

"All right." She stuffed the handkerchief into her pocket. "Well, you know where I'll be if you need me." On her way out, Granny shook the shutters to make sure my window was still locked. Though they were tightly closed, moonlight crept through the slats.

I lay awake listening to the grandfather clock's *tick-tocks* and trying to clear my mind. Although I closed my eyes and started counting sheep, I couldn't stop mulling over my feelings for Peter and my fear that they were unrequited. I couldn't stop distressing about Granny and her baking business and her aching arm. But most of all, I was too afraid of having another Wolfstime nightmare to nod off. Maybe some warm milk would help, like Granny had given me when I was a little girl. Only now, I didn't want to confess to her that I was afraid, so I waited for the sign—her snoring—to know it was safe.

I hopped out of bed and padded through the dark, barricaded cottage, pausing briefly at the living room where Granny lounged on Wolfstime nights. In the rippling glow of candles, I watched her sleep, her glasses crooked on the bridge of her nose and her mouth gaping open. Despite the deadly weapon in her hands and the thunderous wheezes coming out of her every few seconds, she appeared so peaceful.

Ever so quietly, I continued on into the kitchen and heated a cup of milk. Perched on the stool, I sipped it slowly, listening to the alternating sounds of the grandfather clock's *ticktocks* and Granny's snores for what seemed like forever. My gaze eventually landed on the bundles of goodies on the counter. If I wanted to help fill my delivery basket, now was as good a time as any.

Taking Granny's cookbook off the shelf, I started flipping through its pages. And, to my delight, the cookies called for just four ingredients: butter, sugar, flour, and vanilla—all of which Granny had at the ready. Not even *I* could mess up something so simple! After the catastrophe of Peter's birthday cake, I wanted to prove that I really could put any troll, ogre, or princess to shame in the kitchen.

While Granny slept, I tied her apron over my nightgown and went to work as quietly as possible. I had a wonderful feeling that my shortbread cookies would turn out every bit as mouthwatering as hers. Confidence gushed through my veins as I mixed, rolled, and shaped. And, as the first batch baked, its wonderful aroma brought me back to when the neighbor children and I sat by the fireplace, munching on the sugary cookies and listening to Granny read from the storybook.

June, eight years ago

The buttery, sweet smell of cookies wafted through the cottage, and I curled my toes in my stockings as I begged Granny to read another story. The neighborhood children had already come and gone, but as always, I hadn't had enough.

The flames in the fireplace danced as she flipped the pages, finding the story that came after the one she'd read yesterday about the emperor who walked through the town in his undergarments.

"Long, long ago, deep in the Enchanted Forest, there was an exquisite castle, and in it lived King and Queen Nostos."

"Did they have a baby?" I asked. "Was there a prince or a princess?"

Granny peered at me over her glasses. "No, they didn't have a baby, at least none that I know of."

I hid my frown behind a bite of shortbread.

"Every morning before breakfast, the king enjoyed strolling to a nearby spring. He told his wife he liked to listen to the nightingales sing as he washed his hands and face in the clear, cool water. On his birthday, the queen decided to surprise him with a picnic prepared by the royal cook; however, when she arrived at the spring, she discovered something most unsettling.

"The king sat on the shore, where he listened not to birds, but to a fair washerwoman singing as she worked. She had a lovely voice and long, pale-blond hair, and once she filled her basket with cleaned linens, she shed her clothes down to her petticoat and jumped into the clear, cool water.

"The king was so entranced by the woman's beauty that he never noticed the queen's presence. The queen suspected that her husband loved the washerwoman more than she, and she feared losing the power and luxuries that her position entitled her. In a jealous rage, the queen went to an evil sorceress, seeking a curse.

"The next morning, after the washerwoman indulged in her swim, the curse befell her. She could not emerge from the spring. She could not breathe in air, only water."

"Like a fish?" I asked.

"Yes. The temptress was forced to stay in the spring forevermore." Granny let me look at the picture of the beautiful maiden sinking into the spring, surrounded by her long, flowing hair and little bubbles as she reached upward with both arms. She looked so sad, and I wondered if people could actually cry underwater. "The story doesn't end there," Granny said, eventually turning the page.

"The washerwoman wanted revenge on Queen Nostos," she continued reading out loud. "She grew strong in her new home, and with every kick, she slowly and patiently expanded the spring into a pristine, bottomless lake. Soon thereafter, a terrible earthquake—or some storybooks claim it was a giant sinkhole—swallowed the castle in its entirety, towers and all. No one came upon the castle or its inhabitants ever again. As for Lake Nostos, its water was said to magically cure curses."

"What do you mean, Granny?" I asked.

"People believed the lake water could restore things back to the way they were."

"No, what I want to know is: is there a whole castle somewhere under the Enchanted Forest?"

Granny chuckled. "No, child. There's no sunken castle or Lake Nostos. It's all just a fairy tale."

"Fire! Fire!" Granny yelled, throwing open the oven and fanning the cloud of smoke with a dish towel.

I leapt off the stool on which I'd apparently fallen asleep and tried to steady myself on legs that weren't quite awake. As I blinked in the daylight, images of the dream I'd had flashed back to me: the dark, foggy night, the torches, the fire . . . And yet, those things had happened there in Granny's kitchen, and at my own irresponsible hands.

"What in the land are you doing . . ." Granny demanded, using a hot pad to reach into the inferno and bring out a tray of a dozen of what looked like steaming chunks of coal.

"Baking cookies," I said, wiping the wetness off my chin. For a second, I feared it was blood—but thankfully, this time, it was only saliva. "See?" I gestured at the piles of shortbread cookies on the countertop that I'd baked prior to the batch that hadn't survived.

"So you're *not* trying to burn the house down?"

"No, of course not. I am so sorry, Granny. I must have nodded off." I unlocked and opened the windows and then began helping Granny clean up the mess.

As I washed the cookie sheets, I felt Granny staring at me. When I turned in her direction, her bosom rose and fell in a deep sigh, and she said, "Promise me you won't sleep-bake ever again."

Once we had the kitchen put back together and

the majority of the smoke had cleared out the window, Granny collapsed into a chair and exhaled loudly. Most of her curlers had come loose and fallen to the floor, but two or three hung on for dear life.

I moistened a towel and rubbed a black smear off her flushed, wrinkled cheek. "Granny, I was baking these cookies because I wanted to help."

She huffed and snatched the towel away from me, finishing the task herself. "I know."

An hour or so later, after a quick breakfast, I stood among the rusty axes, piles of kindling, muddy boots, fox and rabbit pelts, rucksack, knives, tin bowls, and coils of ropes on Amos Slade's squeaky porch. He was first on my delivery list that day.

"Go away. Unless you have peach pie," he called through the window before I'd had a chance to knock. Amos Slade loved four things most in the land: hunting, his hound dog, playing cards with his rowdy friends, and Granny's peach pie.

"It's too early in the season for peaches. But I have rhubarb, your second favorite," I offered, and thankfully, it was enough to get the cranky bachelor to open the door.

With a grunt, he held out his hand to accept it.

I said, "Would you like a sample of shortbread? There's no charge."

"I suppose so," he said from somewhere behind his thick mustache. He set the pie down on the window ledge and I watched expectantly as he took a bite of the cookie. His eyes narrowed and then protruded as if he were being strangled. To my horror, he started hacking like I'd poisoned him.

"Are you all right, Mr. Slade?"

"That 'cookie' . . . is not meant . . . for human consumption," he stammered between coughs. He threw the remaining half of the cookie off his porch, into the dirt.

"What? They taste just fine," I said, but then I realized

for the first time that I'd been so sidetracked I hadn't even bothered to sample my own goods. I grabbed one out of my basket and took a bite—only I would've had better luck sinking my teeth into a horseshoe. I pulled the cookie out of my mouth and tried not to look as mortified as I felt.

In the midst of my apology, Amos's dog loped across the yard and gobbled up the tossed cookie. Then he leaned back on his hind legs and, though I noticed he kept a safe distance and a watchful eye on me, eagerly begged his old man for another.

Amos raised his gray, bushy brows. "Wait a minute now," he said slowly. "That hound is the pickiest eater I ever met. But I'll be damned; he likes your cookies."

"Would you like to buy some, then?" I ventured, crossing my fingers behind my back.

Amos tilted his head and stared at me for a moment before glancing down at his still-begging dog. His weathered face broke into a smile, and he shook his head. Digging in his pocket, he said, "I'll take half a dozen."

When I got home later that afternoon, I found my grandmother humming and knitting on the living room sofa. "Granny, I have some good news."

"What is it?" she asked, peering up at me over her glasses.

"I sold four dozen dog biscuits today." I dropped the coins in her open palm.

"Dog biscuits?" she asked. "What nonsense are you talking about now?"

"Apparently, my shortbread is inedible for humans, yet irresistible to our customers with four legs and a tail."

"But if folks can barely afford to keep their own mouths fed, why would they buy biscuits for their dogs?"

"You have to go to the right people," I answered. And before she could shut me down, I quickly laid out my plan: "I was thinking that when I'm making my usual rounds, I can give biscuit samples to the customers who have dogs. And if someone says 'That's the silliest thing I've ever heard of!' I'll just smile and say that Mrs. so-and-so thought so, too; but now she doesn't know how her pooch ever lived without Granny's dog biscuits." I bit my lip, waiting for her response.

Granny counted the money, and the tiniest grin appeared on her face. "It's not the worst idea you've ever had."

"So . . . ?"

"All right."

I almost toppled over. "All right? As in, 'we're doing this'?"

"As in, 'you'd better get baking.' And this time, try not to set the whole damn house on fire."

It was probably ridiculous how happy Granny's pat on the back made me feel, but I gladly took it and ran into the kitchen.

Thirteen

After baking and bundling up cookies, pies, buns, and dog biscuits for the next day's deliveries, Granny and I settled in at the table for suppertime. She grimaced when she lifted her arm, even just to mop up the last traces of vegetable stew with her biscuit, and I wished for the hundredth time that Wolfstime had already passed. However, there were three more nights to go.

"I'll batten down the cottage tonight," I offered as I started clearing the dishes. "You just sit here and rest."

"Nonsense. We'll do it together, like we always have."

I knew better than to argue, so I just sighed as I took the bowls and butter back to the kitchen. "Have you ever gone to see Dr. Curtis about your scar?" I asked a moment or two later. "I know you're always saying he's nothing but a kook in fancy britches, but who knows? Maybe he can give you a salve or something that will take away the pain."

"No salve will work for this scar." Granny adjusted the ruffle of her sleeve to completely cover her right wrist. Then she stood, the legs of her chair screeching against the wooden floor. "Unless it was a magic salve," she said with a little snort.

I knew Granny had only jested about the magic salve. However, as we fell into our traditional Wolfstime routine—locking the shutters, boarding up the doors, and pulling the iron grate over the fireplace—I couldn't get the notion of it out of my mind. Could there really be a magic elixir somewhere in the land that would keep Granny's arm from hurting? I'd never met a fairy, witch, sorceress, wizard—or any practitioner of magic, for that matter. They weren't exactly easy to come by—they tended to keep their identities and habitats top secret, and they cast various spells to further ensure their concealment. However, Granny herself told me that my red riding hood had been enchanted by a wizard, and since she'd never ventured far from our village, I guessed he lived nearby.

If I could somehow find that wizard, would he give me a magic salve for Granny?

Later that night, Granny snoozed on the sofa with her crossbow, and I rummaged through the keepsakes I'd collected and stowed beneath my bed through the years. In the far corner sat the box in which Granny had wrapped my red riding hood when she gave it to me for my thirteenth birthday. I slid it out and lifted the lid. As I remembered, I'd put the square of parchment that had been pinned to the hem of the cloak inside the box for safekeeping.

I flopped onto my bed, and by the glow of candles, I examined the note, hoping to find some sort of clue that could lead me to the wizard who'd written it. I ran the tip of my finger over the words: WEAR THIS GARMENT, FEAR NOT THE WOLF.

I didn't recognize the handwriting, and I couldn't detect anything notable about the parchment itself. Disappointed, I set it on my bedside table and curled up on my side, listening to the steady snores wafting from the living room. The grandfather clock struck twelve, and a bolt of energy zapped through my body. It was midnight!

Sitting straight up, I grabbed the wizard's note.

Most folks used ink made of ordinary blueberries— the ones that grew abundantly on bushes in the surrounding forest. But the ink the wizard used was decidedly darker. *Midnight* blue, to be precise. The only thing I could think of that would yield such a dark blue hue was the bilberry.

Once, when I was about ten, Granny asked me to gather berries in the woods. I took my basket and headed off, realizing hours later that I'd gone deeper and farther than I'd ever been. I stopped to drink from a spring and explore a cave, and that's where I found a patch of bilberry shrubs. Only I didn't know them to be any different from blueberries, at the time. I did know that it was nearing suppertime, and I'd best be on my way. So I picked every last berry and tramped home. By the time I walked in the door, I'd eaten all but a handful of the delicious, midnight blue berries. Granny wasn't too pleased with me for being gone so long and having so little to show for it, but she stopped scolding me when she saw the berries.

"Where did you find these, child?" she asked. I was afraid to confess that I'd wandered so very far away, so I shrugged and said I didn't know. "I haven't seen a bilberry since I was a girl. Mama used to use them with apples in pies and pastries. Here, eat it," she said, handing one to me. I didn't dare admit I'd already eaten dozens, so I popped it in my mouth and smiled.

Now I smiled at the note in my hand and made a plan. In the morning, I'd go to where I'd found the bilberry shrubs six years ago. Maybe, with a little luck, I'd find the wizard who enchanted my cloak, and Granny's mysterious scar would ache no more.

The ground drops out from under my feet, melting into sludge. As the earth swallows me, I spread my arms, grasping for something to hold on to. I clutch what feels like a branch, and I'm bathed in relief when it breaks my fall; but as I hang, it bends and cracks.

More branches loom below me, only now I see that they are torches. The farthest ones glow the brightest, and as the flames grow, they ignite the torches above them. The light creeps up the walls, illuminating golden-framed paintings of kings and queens, coats of arms, and elaborate tapestries. The torch just below me ignites. I kick, trying to keep it from burning my soles.

Thursday, May 17

I walked down the road and into the village just as I did on any other typical Thursday morning, but it was all just a show to keep Granny from worrying about my whereabouts while I embarked on my quest to find the wizard. Though Granny was the only person I knew who'd actually met a wizard, I'd heard many tales, and one that seemed to come up time and time again was that their magic always came with a price. So I brought the money I'd been saving for the time when I would leave the village in search of my happy ending. It was all I had, so I hoped it would be enough. With every step, I reminded myself that if it was possible to find the wizard, and if he was able to use magic to help Granny's pain go away, it would be worth every last halfpenny in my wooden box.

When I arrived at the schoolhouse, I hid behind the climbing tree and watched through the window as my schoolmates found their seats. I was glad not to be stuck in there with Violet and her friends, especially after the Tucker incident.

Sadly, Peter's desk was empty. Knowing him, he was just tardy again. As time went on, he seemed to show up later and later. Ever since he'd turned seventeen, I was surprised he came to school at all, though. Granny would approve of his decision to stay in school longer than most people if she ever cared enough to reconsider her opinion of him.

I would've liked seeing Peter from afar, even if it was

just the back of his head. I still wasn't ready to be one-on-one with him, because I feared he'd be able to tell I was falling for him. I'd had enough humiliation and awkwardness to last a lifetime.

"You look as if you're up to no good." The deep voice came from behind me, startling me.

I whirled around, covering my heart with my hand. "Really, Peter. You shouldn't sneak up on people."

"Are you going to tell me where you're off to with your basket and bow? Surely your granny isn't making you skip school to do deliveries." He leaned against the tree and crossed his arms. I couldn't help noticing that his biceps bulged beneath his sleeves, or that he'd left his shirt lace un-cinched and untied, giving me a nice view of his broad, muscular chest.

He tilted his head and squinted his right eye, making me wonder if he'd caught me ogling him. I promptly peeled my gaze off his amazing body and stared down at my boots, feeling the heat rise in my cheeks. "I can't tell you. It's a secret. A secret quest, if you will."

I must have sounded stupid, but I felt stupid standing there with my bright red face, trying to act like he was only a friend to me.

Pulling a sad face, Peter hooked his thumb at the schoolhouse. "Miss Cates will be very disappointed. I'm certain she has a thrilling mathematics lesson planned today."

"You best run inside, then. You've already missed a good ten minutes of it." I straightened my skirt and turned to leave. When I glanced over at the little stone building, I spotted someone peering out the window. "And it looks like somebody is eagerly waiting for you."

His gaze followed mine. "She'll be waiting in vain, then. I'm coming with you, wherever you're going."

I opened my mouth to argue, but as Violet leaned closer to the glass, her hands on her hips, I could only imagine how furious seeing the two of us together made her. Suddenly, skipping school with Peter seemed like the best idea ever, even if attempting to track down a wizard wasn't. "All right, but on one condition."

Smirking, he pushed away from the tree and closed the space between us. "Name it."

"You cannot, under any circumstances, tell a soul where we're going, or what I'm about to do."

"I wouldn't dream of it, Red. Those are the rules of every secret quest—as any given storybook dictates. And I have one condition for you, as well."

"What is it?"

"We have to be back well before sundown. I have to shoe a pair of horses in town, and then Mama's making lamb stew for supper because my papa and I are going after the wolves."

The idea of Peter going out with the hunters made my stomach drop. However, I had to remind myself that boys his age had been part of the Wolfstime hunting parties for many generations. "If I got home after sundown, my granny wouldn't need to worry about the wolves getting me—she'd kill me herself," I said.

Before Peter and I headed into the village, I gave Violet a little wave, and I could tell by the strained look on her face that she was none too happy. We picked our way through the side roads and alleyways until we found ourselves in the bowels of the forest. I kept taking wrong turns, and I began to earnestly question my memory of the place where I'd picked bilberries so long ago.

"Forgive me for asking, Red," Peter said after I'd made him backtrack for the tenth-or-so time, "but have you any inkling as to where we're going?"

"I thought I did. Now I'm not so sure."

"Maybe you should stop and ask for directions."

"What a grand idea," I said. "As soon as you find someone to ask, let me know."

"The only person we'd encounter way out here is one of these bandits," he said, tapping a sun-bleached wanted poster on the trunk of a tree. He then launched into an anti-thief rant worthy of the village soapbox. Though I nodded and made agreeable noises whenever proper, my gut knotted because at the market three days ago, I'd proven that I, too, was nothing better than a two-bit thief.

The brush grew dense, and Peter forged ahead of

me, deftly slicing through the thicket with a branch, as if it were a sharp blade. "Red, come over here. Shhhh."

In a small clearing lay a doe and her twin spotted fawns. Peter stood only a few feet away from their grassy bed, waving me in. Although I tried to be as discreet as humanly possible, the deer sprung up and fled. In the blink of an eye, they plunged deep into the woods and disappeared.

Peter and I walked a while longer, until we found ourselves in a gully. "This little guy wouldn't have a prayer if my brothers were here to capture him," he said, shaking his head at a chubby frog on a log. The instant the frog turned its bulging eyes on me, it promptly hopped away. "My, oh my, Red. You sure have a way with woodland creatures," Peter said. "You're a regular storybook princess."

"Don't be daft," I said. "Animals adore me every bit as much as they do Snow White or Cinderella."

He had a point, though. When we were children, all kinds of critters had been drawn to me. When we'd walked through the forest, bluebirds and butterflies had fluttered above me, and squirrels and rabbits had loped at my feet. In town, horses, cats, and dogs had nudged up to me. Now animals seemed to be fearful or at least wary of me: the squirrel outside my bedroom window, Amos Slade's and Priscilla's dogs, our chickens, and, as Peter had mentioned, the woodland creatures.

I was considering that oddity when it struck me that the spring the frog had jumped into resembled the one I'd taken a drink from on the day I'd discovered the bilberries. Beyond the glistening spring loomed the cave, just as I remembered. My spirits lifted when I spotted the bright green bushes laden with little, round, midnight blue berries. Now that I'd found them, I could only hope the wizard lived nearby.

I set my basket beside the spring. "Have you ever tried a bilberry?" I asked, presenting Peter with a freshly picked handful.

"Can't say that I have." He popped several into his mouth. "They taste like blueberries," he said, smacking his lips and gathering more. "Now, don't get me wrong. These taste great, and I always enjoy a long stroll in the forest with you. Especially in lieu of going to school. But, I have to ask, is this teensy little berry the ultimate goal of this important secret quest of yours?"

He tossed a bilberry high into the air. I tried to catch it in my mouth, but it bounced off my lip and rolled to the ground. "Not quite. Come along." I pulled him away from the shrubs and, holding both of his hands in mine, closed my eyes and took a very deep breath.

"Red? *Hallo*, are you all right?" he asked after a few seconds.

When I opened my eyes, his forehead creased as if he thought I'd toppled off my rocker.

A cool breeze rippled through the leaves. The time had come to tell him. "I'm searching for a wizard. I think he might live around here."

"A wizard? Oh. Well, then, why didn't you say so in the first place?"

"You know how to find a wizard, Peter?" I asked hopefully.

"The only way to find a wizard is if he *wants* to be found. Everybody knows that."

I sighed as I lifted the basket. "I know. I just . . ." I could practically feel the hope draining from my heart and out of my toes. Peter was right.

He tilted his head and grinned. "What's in the basket?" he asked.

"A rhubarb pie for the wizard, and some crumpets for us to snack on when we get hungry." I didn't mention that I'd also brought the box holding my lifetime savings. I knew it would be difficult to hand it over to the wizard, but that was a moot point. I was naïve to honestly believe I ever had a chance of finding a wizard.

"A pretty girl *and* a rhubarb pie? This wizard you seek—he'd be cracked not to want you to find him. I'm shocked he's not right here in his pointy purple hat, tooting a horn and doing a jig." Peter pumped his fists and bent his knees up and down, doing a horrendous little dance.

"Thank you for trying to make me feel better, Peter. But you're right. This quest to find a wizard is ridiculous.

It's like finding a needle in a haystack. I'm sorry I wasted your time." I sighed. "We should just go home."

"Go home." The voice sounded much more gravelly than Peter's.

My heart raced as my eyes darted about, seeking the stranger among us. Oddly, Peter wasn't reacting to the mysterious voice at all; he just danced a couple more seconds and then gave me a blank look.

"Peter, didn't you hear that?" I nocked an arrow and pointed it at the rocky ledge above the cave, where the words had come from. "Tell me you heard it."

"Heard what?" Peter asked. Out of the corner of my eye, I saw him pick up a rock the size of his hand. "What did you hear? Red, tell me what is going on."

"I don't know. I heard a voice. A really . . . I don't know, *peculiar* voice. Somebody is up there!"

"It's probably just a bird, or maybe a bat. Perhaps that frog heard you're a legendary cliff jumper and wanted to show you his skills."

"Peter! I'm being *serious*," I said through the corner

of my lips, keeping my eyes trained on the rock ledge. "Someone is watching us. I heard him speak. He said, 'Go home,' as clear as day." Surely I hadn't imagined it!

A single black feather floated in the air, peacefully and silently. Blowing my hair out of my eyes, I drew my bow as a scruffy bird lifted off from above the cave, flapping and flopping through the air.

"See there? It's only a crow." Peter chuckled. "Though I confess it's a rather dastardly one, so you might want to keep your bow drawn."

Strangely, the bird did not fly away from me like the other woodland critters. Instead, he hovered oafishly just above my hood. Suddenly, his beak opened, and he asked, "You have crumpets?"

My eyeballs practically popped out of my head as I implored Peter, "Please tell me you heard that. The bird is *talking*, Peter!"

Peter blinked a couple of times and said, "It's squawked a time or two, as crows are prone to do. But as for speaking . . ."

I bit my lower lip, knowing full well—and dreading with every ounce of my being—where his train of thought was taking him. If he couldn't hear that the crow was speaking actual human words, he undoubtedly believed I'd suddenly gone stark raving mad. *Was* I going crazy?

"What did the crow say?" Peter asked, his voice hitching.

I swallowed. "Um, I think he wants a crumpet."

"I haven't had one for over three years," the bird squawked.

I turned back to Peter, silently begging him to acknowledge that he'd finally heard the crow speak.

But he only gestured for me to lower my weapon. He shook his head slowly, fixing me with a gaze that was part concern and part fear. "Red, are you all right? What's going on?"

How could it be that he didn't hear the bird speaking actual words? Why was I the only one that could understand him? Unless . . . Maybe the crow belonged to the wizard?

"Take me to the wizard, and I'll give you a crumpet," I whispered to the bird as he swooped by on his tatty wings. He blinked his dark, beady eyes at me and took off.

I packed up my bow, grabbed the basket, and hurried after him, calling, "Come on, Peter!" over my shoulder. Perhaps I was crazy, but I hoped beyond hope that Peter would come along with me on my journey.

Fourteen

The cabin was odd indeed—narrow and lofty, with three small, shutterless windows and a dwarf-sized yellow door. It was built of stones of every color, shape, and size, which gave it the distinct appearance of being crooked. On its roof grew patches of grass and wilting dandelions, and to its side, a little vegetable garden. Out back, a swaybacked white mare swished her tail and gazed at us with her pink eyes.

Without taking my eyes off the rickety dwelling, I reached in my basket for a crumpet and held it out for the crow. He didn't utter a word as he snatched the treat in his beak and perched on a window ledge.

"I don't believe it," said Peter as he, too, gaped at the house. "Do you really think a wizard lives here?"

"Only one way to find out." I dropped the dragon-head knocker against the door and held my breath.

Crashing noises followed by a stream of curses that would make even Granny blush came from inside. The crow continued eating, obviously unfazed. Peter's eyes widened. "Red, I'm not so sure this is a good idea. He sounds like a regular lunatic."

"He very well might be crazy, but I have something very important to ask him," I replied. "We've come this far, Peter. Please, stay with me just a little longer."

The little yellow door finally cracked open, revealing mid-chest and downwards of a knobby man in a shirt that once upon a time might have possibly been white, baggy brown trousers, and bare feet with hairy toes. He ducked and stepped out, letting us see the top of him: wild yellowish-white hair for his head, brows, and beard, and a long, thin nose that angled down. Clearly, the man's bloodshot eyes were struggling to adjust to the sunlight, and his knees were having a hard time keeping his body from falling over.

"That's no wizard," Peter whispered in my ear. "It's just an eccentric old drunkard."

"Did you really think he'd be wearing a pointy purple hat, Peter?" I whispered back. Though I had to hand it to my friend; the man looked—and smelled—more like a washed-up toper than a powerful wizard. I smiled at the man and started to ask if he'd like a rhubarb pie. However, he didn't give me a chance to.

"Will you look at that, Heathcliff? Look, look, look," the man said, his bony fingers reaching out for my face. "It's uncanny!" I stepped back, tripping on a gray cat that I hadn't seen.

"What do you mean?" I asked, starting to feel panicky. "Who's Heathcliff, and what's uncanny?"

"Where, oh, where are my manners?" he said, retracting his hands to open the door wider. "Oh, here they are, right where I left them." He pantomimed pulling something out of his pocket and putting it in his mouth. After clearing his throat, he continued, "Allow me to introduce myself. My name is Knubbin."

I'd never met a wizard before, so I didn't know how to properly greet him. I decided to give him a little curtsy. "I'm Red. At least, that's what everybody calls me."

"I know," he said, curtsying back.

I blinked, trying to wrap my mind around the wizard's odd welcome. It took me a moment to realize I hadn't finished our introductions. "This is Pe—"

"You've come all this way," the wizard interrupted. "The least I can do is offer you a chair and some tea. Come in. Please do!"

Peter and I exchanged hesitant looks. Then Peter gestured for me to go ahead, and so I did.

"Allow me to clarify in the clearest manner I know," the man said, blocking Peter's way. "You, my poppet, can come in. The boy can sit . . . over yonder." He twirled his bony finger in the air, and next pointed at a flat-topped rock by the garden.

"That's not going to happen," Peter said sternly, folding his arms over his chest.

"It's a very comfortable sitting place," Knubbin said. "I sit there myself for hours on end, watching my carrots grow. Once I thought I'd watch the cabbage grow, but there's nothing quite as boring as cabbage, so I guess you could say I learned my lesson. But the poppet and I won't be long at all, so you have nothing to worry about, unless, of course, you have something to worry about. And that would be quite worrisome, don't you agree?"

Peter said, "What I mean is, I'm not letting her go in alone."

"She won't be alone, my dear oblivious boy. She'll be with *me*." The man stroked his beard as he turned to face me. "Correct me if I'm incorrect, but aren't you here to see a wizard?"

"You *are* a wizard, aren't you?" I asked. "The one who enchanted my red riding hood?"

He blinked several times, seemingly chewing on my words. "Well! *Of course* I'm a wizard. Did you not hear me introduce myself? Knubbin is my name. *Am I a wizard?* What kind of *ridiculous* question is that? And equally ridiculous—I might add, if I were to add something, which I am—is your ignorance on the topic at hand." He wiggled his hand in my face and briefly smirked before going on. "Only the person seeking the wizard may speak with him. Wizards do not accept audiences when it comes to matters of magic."

"So you are the one who put a spell on this?" I repeated, opening the side of my cape.

"Ah, it has held up quite nicely, if I *do* say so myself. But if I do say so myself, I risk sounding like a braggart, don't you think? *Shhh*, don't answer that, it will only hurt my feelings, and then I'll have no choice but to ask you to leave my premises, never to return."

"Oh, no, it's definitely held up. Thank you."

"You are welcome. So, my poppet, where were we?" He looked down at our feet. "Of course, silly me. We are outside, on my stoop. And the reason we're still out here is because you have a choice to make. Now, choose wisely, because unwise choices have destroyed many a wise creature. One, you can come in and the two of us— no more, no less—will chitchat." His lips curved into an impish grin. "Two, you and your beau can be off, lickety-split." He frowned and waved as if someone was headed down the path. "So what will it be? Oh, the suspense . . ." he said, rubbing his hands together.

I met Peter's eyes and smiled in a way I hoped made me appear brave and self-assured.

"I will wait in the garden," Peter offered slowly, "if that's what you want, Red." His gaze darkened as he turned to Knubbin. "As for you, Wizard, if you so much as touch one hair on her head—"

"Touch a *hair on her head*?" The wizard repeated, looking like he'd licked a lemon. "Gracious, why would I ever do *that*?"

Peter's forehead creased, and I bet I appeared equally confused.

"Of course! I know the answer," Knubbin piped up, tapping his finger on his cheek. "I do, on rare occasion, require a strand of human hair in order to do a little magic. But in that particular case, I would ask nicely for it. Or perhaps I'd take one she'd shed and carelessly left behind. But I can assure you, as I'm assuring myself just now, I will not touch her hair whilst it is still attached to her scalp."

Peter grabbed my shoulders and pulled me close, whispering gruffly in my ear, "Listen, Red. This so-called wizard is as mad as a March hare. I don't think this meeting is a good idea—"

"Excuse us, Knubbin," I said, and tugged Peter around the corner of the house to speak in semiprivate. "Don't worry so much. He said he wouldn't touch a hair on my head, and I believe him. I'll be fine, Peter. Please, we've come this far. It will only take a few moments."

He flexed his jaw and looked away, at the garden. "All right, but I'll be right here."

I thanked Peter and followed the wizard into his cabin, which was surprisingly—even miraculously—spacious, given the outside. Candles flickered from almost every nook, and yet my eyes needed a few moments to adjust to the dimness. The place stunk of dust and wet dog, so the lack of light was probably a blessing. Like the front door, the furniture appeared shrunken yet sturdy. Pans and plates cluttered the kitchen, a mountain of kindling buried the potbellied stove, and small statues of dragons, lions, and wolves were arranged on a curio shelf. A long black cloak dangled from a coatrack, and on the wall beside it hung a childlike painting of a crescent moon and stars.

"Well, don't just stand there," Knubbin said. "Hang your riding hood on the rack and sit and have a drink or three."

"I'm not thirsty, but thank you all the same," I said, taking my hood off my head as I lowered myself into a small armchair. From there, I could see the window where the crow perched—also the one closest to where Peter waited. He paced back and forth alongside the garden. I had the feeling his heart was thumping against his ribs, as was mine.

"Suit yourself, poppet. I will have some mead if you don't mind. Don't get up, I'll help myself. Lucky for the both of us, I know exactly where I left it, which is not always the case, in case you were curious. And I'll take a wager that you are the curious sort, or else you wouldn't be here, would you?"

Once he joined me in the living room, I said, "I'm here to ask for something magical." Suddenly, my granny's warning from so long ago came back to haunt me: "Even when magic is used for good, it can become something very bad." Her words gave me a moment of hesitation, but I was determined to see this through. How could wanting Granny to be well be a bad thing?

"I know why you're here," said Knubbin as he settled opposite me and crossed his legs. He looked rather unwieldy, a spindly giant sitting on a tiny sofa. "I know everything, you know. Everything there ever was to know is right in here," he said, tapping the side of his bristly brow.

"You don't know everything." When I glanced at the window, I couldn't see Peter any longer. I presumed he finally took a seat on the rock, and I didn't blame him one bit. "You thought Peter was my beau. He's not. We've been friends since we were children. We're only friends."

"Not your beau, you say?" He took a swig out of his cup and cracked a yellow-toothed smirk. "If you truly believe that, it seems to me that I am more familiar with your heart than you. However, you're not here for a silly old love potion—that much is clear. It does have something to do with your heart, though. There's something tormenting it, is there not? And, if my suspicions are correct, this something is most agonizing . . ." He brought his hands together, creating the shape of a ball. Light glowed from the center of his palms—or at least I thought it had, but perhaps it was only a trick played on me by the flicker of a candle and the flit of my eyelashes. ". . . when the moon is full."

"Yes, exactly!" I straightened my posture, thrilled that this rumpled tippler was finally beginning to sound like a true man of magic. He knew of Granny's Wolfstime aches even without me having mentioned it!

He quaffed his mead and then let out a horrible burp. "How long have you been having them?"

Just like that, my hopes of him being somewhat sane

went up in smoke. "I'm sorry, but what in the land are you talking about?"

"The nightmares."

I gasped. "You know about my dreams? But, how?"

"You take after your mother, you know. If I were to guess, I'd say she'd been younger than you by a good two or three years when she came to me." He closed his eyes and rubbed his temples. "Ah, there it is. The hesitant knock on my door. Standing in the doorway, she tells me her name . . . Annette? Anna? No, that's not quite right . . ."

"Anita," I supplied.

"Anita, yes. Her big, pretty eyes imploring me to make the terrible dreams stop. She doesn't know what they mean, and she's afraid. She says she'll do anything. . . ."

My world tilted, and I found myself gasping for my next breath. "Wait, what? My mother had the Wolfstime dreams, too? *You knew my mother?*"

"Of course I did." He pressed his lips together, looking as if he were offended. "In fact, she sat precisely where you are sitting, only a smidgen to the right. Or was it to the left? Oh! And that is from me. From me, to her." His bony finger pointed at the gold cross pendant dangling from my neck, coming close enough to almost touch it—but then pulled back, as if it had burnt him. "So pretty, and yet so powerful."

I put my hand over the cross, pressing it into my collarbone. *Powerful?* "Does my cross have magic? Did you enchant it to make her dreams stop?"

"Stop the dreams? No, no, no. That would be far too dangerous. I would *never* stop anyone's dreams." He paused and stroked his long beard. "Well, 'never' is a strong word, and I try never to use it—because, you see, with magic, there is always a way around, or over, or sometimes right straight through 'never' into the vastness of possibility," Knubbin said, fluttering his bony fingers like raindrops down to his lap.

"So you didn't help her," I said flatly. It made sense that he had turned her away, because if the cross had been enchanted to keep the Wolfstime dreams away, wouldn't it have worked for me when I wore it, too?

"Oh, but I did help her. Let me ask you this: what are dreams?"

"I'm afraid I'm not the best person to ask. Mine are not like other people's."

"Well, of course they aren't! We are our truest selves when we are dreaming, are we not? When we are awake, we allow outside influences to come in; whereas, when we're fast asleep," he said, lowering his voice as he walked over to the window where the crow dozed, "we allow ourselves to explore the deepest, darkest caverns of our character. In our dream world, the outside world has no power over us. We are truly, irrevocably free!"

With that, he pounded the window ledge. The loud noise made both the bird and me jump. The crow squawked and flew off without a hint of grace. A few of his feathers floated down onto the wood planks. When the wizard crossed the floor and reclaimed his seat across from me, one feather remained stuck to his bare foot.

"When your mother begged me to make her dreams

stop, I asked her if it was the dreams that frightened her, and she pondered my query for quite some time. The clever girl said that the dreams themselves didn't frighten her, it was *not understanding the dreams* that frightened her." He grinned. "Lo and behold, when something scares us, it's usually a simple case of mystification."

"How did you help her?" I asked.

"I cast a spell on the cross pendant to help her demystify her dreams. But that wasn't enough for her, no, no, *no*. She wanted it all to happen sooner, rather than later. Your mother was clever, yet she was impatient. I cautioned her that when she wore the pendant, the dreams would grow more and more intense—they might even drive her to madness. But she assured me that she was strong enough to handle them, come what may. Apparently, she was in quite a rush to realize her true self." His gaze flashed from me to the little statues on his curio.

"Tell me, did your spell work?" I asked, hoping to keep his thoughts from straying beyond the point of no return.

"You tell *me*. Does it?"

I touched the cross. It always made me feel closer to my mother, but I'd never imagined that it was magical. "My Wolfstime dreams are definitely intense, but I'm afraid I'm nowhere near understanding them. If anything, they're more confusing than ever."

"Just be a little more patient," he said very softly, as if only to himself. Then, almost too loudly, "Fetch me some more drink, poppet. In the jug, by the sink."

Rushing, I did as I was told, and then begged him to tell me more. "What was my mother like? Please, I want to hear everything—every last detail."

The wizard uncrossed his legs, furrowed his brows as if in deep thought, and then crossed his legs again the other way. I sat at the edge of my seat, eager to hear more about my mother.

Fifteen

"Anita only came to me once," the wizard said, scratching his knee. "One time, that was it. After that, I never saw your mother again. And then, some twenty years later, your grandmother came to me again, this time for magic to protect you from the wolves. Your grandmother told me the tragic news about your parents, may their souls rest in peace."

"My granny had come to you before, then?"

"I'm afraid my manners have slipped away yet again," the wizard said. "I've been doing all the talking. Now it's your turn." He took a big swig then set the cup down. "Tell me why you are here, poppet. If not for the nightmares, then what is it you want?"

I blinked a few times, not ready to move on when I hadn't yet learned enough. However, I had the distinct feeling that I had to play the wizard's game. "My grand-mother. Her arm aches during the full moon. She has a scar there, and I don't know much about it, but I know it hurts worse each Wolfstime. I can't bear to see her wince in pain, Knubbin. It hurts when she's knitting and when she's cooking. Sometimes it hurts so badly she has to take poppy dust in order to sleep. I'm here for a salve that will take away her pain. Please, will you help me?"

"Let me get this straight," he said, pointing his finger at the rafters. "You've come all this way . . ." He placed his hands, palm sides up, on his lap. ". . . for a pain relief salve?"

"That's right."

The wizard balled his hands into fists. "It never occurred to you to use an herbal ointment, like the rest of the villagers do when they have aches and pains?"

"Yes, of course. Granny said they don't work, though— not even a little bit. Hers is not an ordinary injury, she told me. I've come to you for a magic salve." I smiled and peeked at him through my fluttering eyelashes—like I'd seen Violet and her friends do countless times, whenever they wanted someone to do them a courtesy.

Knubbin inclined his head and quirked his mouth, making me believe the eyelash trick was working and that I finally had something to thank those wicked girls for. "Have you something in your eye, poppet?"

"Oh." I abruptly stopped fluttering and bit my bottom lip. "I must have. But it's fine now. Probably just a pesky little gnat or something."

"I see," the wizard said, before his eyes glazed over and he started muttering a stream of nonsensical words. He became a ventriloquist without a marionette, and had I not needed the magic salve for Granny, I would've run out of the strange little cabin as fast as my legs would carry me. Still babbling, he stood and meandered into the kitchen where he helped himself to some more drink, sloshing it out of the cup as he picked his way back to the chair.

"Pardon me for saying so, but maybe you've had enough to drink?" I asked.

Finally, Knubbin let out a liquor-stenched sigh and said crisply, "The ripple effect of magic never ceases to amaze me."

"How do you mean?" I asked, and he jolted to attention as if he'd forgotten I was there.

"Your grandmother longed to forget the night the wolf killed her husband. It had scarred her. The memory was much too painful, as I'm sure you can imagine. Weeks after witnessing her dear husband's gruesome death, the young Widow Lucas came rapping on my door, distraught and desperate. Ultimately, I made a forgetting potion for her, one that would completely wipe out her memory of that fateful night. Like—*poof!*—it never, ever happened. It's one of my finest spells, if I do say so myself. And I do! Once she drank it, she knew her husband had perished, but had no inkling what had actually happened to him. She seemed better off that way, and went along with her life." After pausing to breathe, he asked, "Are you certain you don't want a drink?"

"Yes, I'm sure. Thank you. And I'm sorry, but I'm confused. You're telling me my grandmother took a forgetting potion, and yet she remembers what happened that night. She's told me."

"Yes, I know she remembers. Now, if you'd only stop interrupting me, perhaps it will all make sense in the end. Or maybe it won't. *Hmmm*, where was I?" With his pointer finger, he thumped the side of his head. "Oh, yes. A notch over three years ago, when your grandmother came seeking magical protection for you—that red cloak you wear—she had to make an enormous sacrifice. You see, I told her that she couldn't help you to her fullest unless her memories were intact—*all* of her memories, especially those that were most painful. I told her this as well as a warning that sometimes, when I'm asked to undo a memory spell, that which we desired to forget in the first place comes back even more acutely. The scar on your grandmother's arm that you speak of, has she ever mentioned how long she's had it?"

I shook my head. "Just that it's from long ago, when she was a young woman. But it's only been the past few years that I've noticed it giving her so much pain." It would've been since around the time she'd given me the cloak for my thirteenth birthday, and the realization made me gasp out loud.

"I suspect that the scar on her arm is a physical manifestation of the scarring and pain she holds in her heart."

"I feel terrible!"

"Love is sacrifice," Knubbin whispered, as if he were reading words written on the wall behind my head. "And so is magic. You see, magic always comes with a price."

I took a deep breath, more determined than ever before to help Granny. "So I've heard. And I assure you, I haven't come empty-handed."

As I lifted the wooden box out of my basket and handed it to him, I forced a smile and tried to keep my lower lip from quivering. His hand plunged into the coins. "Hmmm," he said, creating a waterfall of gold and silver as he dropped them back into the box. The way he played with them put a lump in my throat. Part of me wanted to take the box back from him, tell him I'd made a mistake. The only reason I didn't was my hope of helping Granny—and faith that the wizard would come through for us. "Is this *all*?" he asked, eyeing my basket.

"Actually, there is more." I took the pie out and placed it on the table between us. "It's my granny's specialty. Only, to be fair, I should warn you: one bite and you'll be hooked."

He leaned over and took a whiff with his long, narrow nose. "Ahhh, yes, that smells scrumptious! What is it made of?"

"Rhubarb, flour, sugar, and butter—all the very freshest and finest. She has a secret ingredient as well, but I'm not allowed to tell."

Stroking his beard, he shook his head. "So this secret ingredient, is it gold? Diamonds or, perchance, a dazzling red ruby?"

"Well, no. It's a *pie*."

"Then, I'm sorry, but you haven't given me enough. We will consider this a good faith payment, how's that? Yes, I do like the sound of that."

"Oh," I said, trying not to sound deflated. "I can bring you more pies, if you please. Apple, cherry, and in a few more weeks, peach. Or if pies aren't your thing, how about—"

A cuckoo clock chirped once, twice. "Up, up, up. And out, out, out. Time for you to be on your way, poppet. I'm a very busy man." The wizard sprung out of his seat and gestured for me to do likewise.

"But what about the salve?" I asked, staying put. "What about my poor grandmother?"

"Next time, bring me something more valuable than a box full of coins and a pie full of rhubarb, and perhaps I will have something for you as well."

I bit back a curse, but I couldn't stop my blood from boiling. Pulling my shoulders back and lifting my chin, I said as calmly as possible, "With all due respect, Knubbin, that 'box full of coins' is quite valuable. I've been making deliveries for my granny since I was ten, and on rare occasions, folks will give me an extra halfpenny or two. I've been saving money for the day I leave the village."

"Ah, so it's your runaway stash," he said from the kitchen, where he filled his cup yet again.

"No, that isn't it at all. I'm not running away," I said. "I want to go off into the world and have adventures."

"Po-tay-to, pa-tah-to," he singsonged.

My fingertip grazed the golden cross. "My parents died too young. They didn't get to see the world. And as for my grandmother, she's lived her entire life in the village—most of her years in the same little cottage. Don't you see? She's afraid to leave. I don't want to be like my granny! I want to see new places. I want to meet new people. I want to find my happy ending. And this, right here," I said, collecting the coins the wizard had dropped on the table and putting them back into the box. "This is my *future*. What can be more valuable than that?"

"Fine." He poured the coins into a leather pouch that hung from his belt and handed me the wooden box.

Tilting my head, I waited for him to explain himself. "So you'll do it? You'll make a magic salve for my granny?"

"Come back at high noon tomorrow. Heathcliff will collect you—and only you, this time—from the gully, as it happened today." The crow squawked from his perch at the window as the old man pushed me out the door.

I saw no sign of Peter, and my heart pounded. "Where's my friend?" I asked.

"Heathcliff will make sure you find your way to the boy. I've erased your beau's memory of ever having come here—it's an irksome, yet necessary, precaution. Unless you want him to think you mad, like the villagers think of your grandmother, I warn you to never speak of our meeting." And then the old man slammed the door.

Sixteen

"All right. Thank you. I'll see you again tomorrow,"
I told Heathcliff. He merely blinked his beady eyes at
me, as if he'd forgotten that he was a talking crow. When
he circled in the sky above the cave and flew off, I felt my
hopes flying away with him.

I wanted to have faith that Knubbin could make me
a magic salve that would cure Granny's pain, but in his
drunken state, would the old man even remember my
visit? Even if he did, how could I be sure he wasn't just a
washed-up wizard turned thief? How could I be certain
I'd ever see him again?

Despite my frustration and disappointment, I smiled
when I spied Peter. He sat leaning against a tree, where

he must have nodded off, dreaming about something that made his nose wiggle. I scooped water from the spring and splashed him awake.

He started—and when he saw that I was the culprit, he laughed and put his hands behind his head. "How long have I been snoozing?" he asked with a yawn. His drowsy eyes reminded me of when he was a little boy: glossy with a dash of mischief. True to the wizard's words, Peter seemed to have no recollection of having ventured past this very spot. In his mind, he'd just drifted off for an afternoon nap.

It would be difficult to keep my meeting with the wizard from Peter. And yet, if it meant getting the magic for Granny and also the possibility of learning more about my family, perhaps it was a secret worth keeping.

"I'm almost finished picking bilberries," I said. "Then we'd best be headed back to the village."

With Peter munching on a crumpet and I on bilberries, we made our way through the forest and down the road. When we crossed through the village, an upbeat song wafted from the tavern, and Peter suddenly grabbed my hand and tugged me into the alley, scattering a clowder of cats.

"Peter! What in the land has gotten into you?" I asked as he snatched my basket and set it on some steps.

"Music. Come on, Red, let's dance!" He bowed grandly and I scrunched my nose and shook my head.

"I don't know how," I said. Sad, but true. Most girls had a father or a grandfather, or even an uncle, to teach them the steps. But I only had Granny, and her jig was bad enough to make a pig run away squealing.

"Come on, I'll show you. What are you afraid of? No one will see. Don't be a chicken." Once he turned his big brown eyes on me, I was a goner.

I couldn't really say what my feet were doing, because they seemed so far away from the rest of my body. All I knew was we were stepping, gliding, dipping, and twirling—and all the while, my cheeks ached from grinning. As his fingers curled around my hand, my knees went weak. And yet, I knew Peter wouldn't let me fall. Suddenly, his body brushed against mine. In reality, I'd been pressed against his warm, muscular chest for only a second; but in my world, the instant had lasted much longer—long enough for my heart to skip a beat, my cheeks to blush, and our eyes to meet, merely inches apart. Somehow, I must have kept dancing, because Peter smiled at me like nothing was wrong. He smiled at me like everything was right.

Once the song came to an end, we broke apart, laughing. Some of the villagers had paused to watch us, and I knew Granny would be worrying about where I was, but in that moment, I didn't care.

Peter handed me my basket. "Thanks, Red. That was fun, but I'm sure you think I need to practice a little more before the ball."

His words slugged me in the gut like a sack of potatoes, and I felt a horrible prickling behind my eyes. I hated myself for being so vulnerable. Turning away from him, I swiped away the tears with the back of my hand and started walking home.

"Red, what's wrong?" he asked, jogging to catch up. "Did I step on your toe?" he asked with a chuckle.

I came to a halt and drew a ragged breath. Despite my blinks, a tear rolled down my cheek—so big, warm, and salty, it seemed as if it had been inside of me for a long, long while.

When he studied my face, Peter's smirk vanished. "Oh, no. Red, what is it?"

I hated that he was seeing me cry—and I hated a lot of other things at that moment, as well. "I hate that you're going to the Forget-Me-Not ball, all right? I thought we'd agreed to go to the swimming hole together that night. You said you *loathed* the idea of folks parading around in fancy gowns and britches, putting on airs, pretending to be princes and princesses, when none of us will ever actually see the inside of the royal castle, which is dripping with luxuries that our hard-earned wages afford them."

I paused to wipe another tear, and another. "And speaking of pretending, I think you're pretending that you don't fancy Violet, when it's obvious that you do!

You're delighted that it worked out that you two are coupled up for the first dance."

"You don't honestly believe that, do you? Because, if you remember, I explained why that happened. I gave my word, and I never go back on it—even if it's to Violet."

"Why did you kiss her, then? Of all the girls in the land, why the cruelest one we know?"

Peter scratched under his collar as if he'd been bitten by fleas. "Actually, she kissed me. It took me by complete surprise, I—"

"Oh." I whirled around and began walking again. Somewhere in the cyclone of emotions that brewed inside of me, I think I might have felt a gust of relief.

"Red, wait." He touched my shoulder, and I wriggled away. "I understand that it's confusing. I'm confused, too. However," he said after taking a deep breath, "I don't think it's fair that you're upset with me."

"Because we're 'just friends,' and I have no right to be jealous? Don't you think I know that, Peter?"

"No. Because you kissed Tucker. After that day we went sledding at the church . . ." He pinched the bridge of his nose. "I can't believe you'd do that. Why?"

I swallowed hard and stared down at the road. We were almost to my house. Part of me wanted to run there as fast as I could and not look back at the mess I'd made.

"You can tell me anything, Red. Please, help me understand."

"Tucker knows a secret about me, and . . . I just had to, that's all." I stroked the tail of my braid and sighed miserably.

"What secret?"

I didn't know which would be worse: not being forthright, and having Peter distrust me—maybe even stop being my friend—or confessing the true and shameful reason I kissed Tucker Williamson. How could I admit that I was a thief? I didn't want Peter to look at me the way he looked at the bandits on the wanted posters. I didn't want to let him down, like his favorite uncle had. Neither alternative was bearable! "I can't tell you, Peter. I'm sorry. Truly, I am."

He shoved his hands in his pockets, and a few

moments later, crossed the path leading to my cottage. "Thanks for the crumpet. I guess I'll see you around."

I reached into my quiver. "Take this with you tonight," I said, handing Peter the silver-tipped arrow he'd made for me five years ago. "It's never been shot. I keep it on hand in case of an emergency."

He waved it away. "You keep it," he said.

"No, please. I want you to have it."

"I said no."

"Oh. All right," I said as brightly as I could. "Well, be careful, Peter."

With a heavy heart, I trudged the rest of the way home while Peter returned to town to shoe some horses. Yes, I was alone—but I felt *really* alone—like the difference between a dark night and the darkness in one of my Wolfstime dreams.

When I glimpsed Granny rocking on the porch, brandishing her knitting needles, I tried to switch from my heartache for Peter to my love for the woman who'd sacrificed so much to protect me from the wolves.

Yet somehow, something didn't feel right. Granny seemed more on edge than ever before, and I had the horrible feeling that I was in for a doozy of a lecture. "Where have you been?" she demanded.

I said, "After school I picked some bilberries," and it wasn't a lie. I had gone to school, I just never went in. "I know you love them, and I thought you could make some tarts." But when I opened my basket and placed a little pile of berries on the table beside her, she didn't even glance at it.

"Oh, those are pretty," I said about the jar of wild-flowers adorning the table. "I didn't see those before. Did you pick them yourself?" It had been a long while since Granny had picked flowers.

"Your friends came by to bring them to you. They assumed that since you weren't at school, you were home sick." Her knitting needles stilled as she waited for my response.

"Friends?" My belly lurched with the realization of who the so-called friends were, and how their pretending to be worried about me had all but forced me into the gallows.

"I'll ask you again—and this time, don't you dare fib to me," Granny said. "Where have you been?"

I lowered myself in the chair next to her and sighed. "I'm sorry, Granny. I just didn't feel like going to school. It's such a pretty day, and I didn't want to waste it sitting in a dingy old schoolhouse. I'll do all of my makeup work, don't worry."

"So you're telling me you took the day off school and went to pick bilberries all alone?"

I bit my bottom lip and confessed, "Not alone. I was with . . . a friend." I hoped he was still my friend.

"A boy?" Granny stopped knitting altogether and fixed me with a surly stare.

It seemed like the more I opened my mouth, the deeper the hole I was digging for myself, and I had a feeling that if I told her I'd been with Peter all day, I might as well have started digging that hole six feet into the ground. Actually, hiding in a hole didn't sound like a bad idea. "Um . . ."

"I've heard whispers of your escapades with boys, and I hoped and prayed they were unfounded. I refused to believe that my very own granddaughter would throw herself all over boys, like a good-for-nothing hussy." As her words stung my ears and tears pricked the backs of my eyes, she shook her head at me as if I was something a mutt had dug up in the back corner of an alley.

"It's not true, Granny." It came out like the feeblest of utterances.

"It isn't, is it? Then why does it sometimes take you four hours to make two hours' worth of deliveries?"

"I told you, sometimes I go for a dip in the swimming hole, or—"

"When I send you off to take goods to the villagers, I mean *baked* goods. And what you were doing with the miller's son at market, while I was busy trying to talk some sense into the villagers? Speaking of market, how did you buy all the flour and sugar and fruit, and still have enough money for chickens?"

"Granny, calm down. Please, you've got it all wrong! Those girls who came by are not my friends." I picked up the jar and tossed the flowers into the bushes. "They're trying to put disgusting ideas in your head. Who are you going to trust, *them*, or your own flesh and blood?"

"Your mother liked to run off and do who-knows-what with boys, too, and I won't be making the same mistakes I made with her, with you. I wasn't born yesterday. I know you've been sneaking out and around, and I won't tolerate this despicable behavior—not while you're living under this roof."

Her words hit me like a slap in the face, and I flinched. "Then it's a good thing I'm leaving this stupid little village," I managed to say. "That way, you won't have to worry about me acting like a hussy, or any other vile story someone makes up about me. You won't have to worry about me soiling your reputation. Oh, don't worry about me, Granny. I'll get along just fine without you. What, did you think I'd be your delivery girl all my life?"

"If you keep on this path, the only job you'll be suited for is a tavern girl. Until then, you should do some hard time, thinking about what kind of woman you intend to be."

Thankfully, I was able to grab my basket, run to my room, and slam the door before the tears spilled down my cheeks. "I can't wait to be done with this stupid village once and for all," I shouted as I took the wooden box out of the basket. The box felt as empty as I did. I threw it onto my bed and paced the length of my room. How could I leave, now that I'd given every last halfpenny to the wizard?

How can Granny believe I am nothing more than a harlot?

And how *dare* Violet and her friends come here and put all sorts of disgusting ideas into my grandmother's head! I had finally felt like I'd won a battle against Violet, since she saw Peter and me skipping school together, but then she had to go and bring me flowers. Once again, I was in the loser's circle.

Priscilla might have had a point so long ago in the school yard—that the best vengeance is forever being the bigger person—but after everything Violet had done to me, how much longer could I refrain from setting her flowing ebony curls on fire?

Speaking of fire, my blood was boiling and my room

stifling. I desperately needed to get some fresh air. I heard Granny banging around in the kitchen, so I made a beeline for the front door. The tree swing beckoned me, like it had hundreds of times when I was younger. Gripping the ropes with all of my might, I swayed back and forth like a pendulum, higher and higher, desperately trying to dry my tears and clear my head.

I pointed my toes, closed my eyes, and held back my head, letting the wind sweep my face and tousle my hair. The sensation brought me back to my Wolfstime dreams. In my mind's eye, I saw the full moon—and in my heart, I felt its power.

Footsteps fell fast and heavy on the path. *Someone is coming.* Though I wanted to stay tucked away in my daydream, I began nudging myself into alertness.

For some reason—and perhaps nothing more than stupid optimism—my heart swelled with the hope that Peter had come to smooth everything out between us. If I looked over my shoulder to find him behind me, his beautiful eyes full of remorse and his muscular arms outstretched, surely I would tell him the truth—that I was the very criminal he most detested, a common thief. I'd tell him that I wanted to be a better person, and though I didn't know how, I would someday pay my debts back, and make everything right again.

When I saw the incorrigible Hershel Worthington making his way toward our cottage, I felt like I'd opened up my mouth for a fine custard only to have been fed a rotten egg.

"So we meet again, missy," the tax man said. "It appears you're having a lovely time on that swing."

"Appearances can be deceiving," I said, dragging my feet in the dirt to break my momentum.

"Is your grandmother home?"

"She's inside, probably building a cage," I mumbled. Mr. Worthington raised his bushy eyebrows questioningly, but then Granny grabbed his attention.

"I'm right over here, if you could see past that outlandish feather in your cap," she snapped. She stood on the front porch with her hands on her hips. She was so near, and yet I felt as if we weren't even in the same land.

"Ah, Widow Lucas," he said as his enormous black boots clunked up the steps. "I trust you were expecting me. May I come in?"

"If you must." She shooed him into the house and slammed the door shut.

Wanting to hear their conversation, I jumped off the swing and jogged around the house to the back door. I slipped into the cottage, where I expected to see Granny handing off the money—counted down to the last halfpenny—and unceremoniously booting the tax man out. On the contrary, Granny stood silently quaking in his menacing shadow. I tucked myself behind the grand-father clock, where I could spy on them without being spotted.

"It's all here," the tax man said, trying to hand her an official-looking scroll. However, she only stared with glazed eyes, so he placed it on the table. "You have no choice but to relinquish your cottage. You and your granddaughter have three days in order to pack your personal possessions and seek alternate residence. Our benevolent ruler apologizes for the inconvenience, and sends from the royal castle his best wishes for a prosperous season." He gave her a little bow, scooping his hat in the air.

What just happened? *Relinquish our cottage? Three days to seek alternate residence?*

My mouth fell open, and I backed into the wall to steady myself. How could he do that to us? It made no sense. Granny had said there was nothing to worry about. He'd given her an extension. At no point had she mentioned even the teensiest possibility of *losing* the cottage.

Once Mr. Worthington said, "Good day, Widow Lucas," and slammed the front door, I stepped out from behind the clock.

Granny heaved a sigh that could have snuffed out a dozen candles. She rubbed her palms together, and without looking up at me, said, "Well, that nasty business is taken care of. I'm happy to say Hershel Worthington granted us three more days to come up with the money.

Nice man, really. Very agreeable. Just doing his job. And now, I'd best do mine." Then she stalked into the kitchen.

I couldn't believe it! Surely Granny hadn't outright lied to me. Why would she say the tax man gave her three more days to pay? With my own ears, I'd heard him say we had to be packed and out of our cottage by then.

If I'd only known we were in danger of losing our home, I could have offered the tax man my life's savings—and if it wasn't enough, perhaps it would buy us a little more time, for real. But now it was impossible, since I'd given every bit of my money to a drunken old wizard! For a second, I wondered if I could get the payment back from Knubbin—perhaps tell him I'd come back for the magic salve as soon as I'd scrounged up the money again.

However, Knubbin told me to come back the next day at noon, and I knew deep inside that I'd never be able to find him when he wasn't yet ready to be found. It was hopeless! I held my stomach, trying to control the waves of nausea.

And then I heard a sound that pierced right through my heart. I walked into the kitchen, where I saw my crumpled granny in front of the pantry. She was on her knees, sobbing.

I'd never seen Granny cry.

That was when I realized she'd lied to me because she was too proud to admit that she couldn't pay her debt. Granny's shoulders shook and her hands covered her face. She must have heard the floor creak under my weight, because she suddenly looked over at me. Her glasses were wet and smeared. "I'm sorry, child," she murmured.

"There has to be something we can do," I said. "The king doesn't just go around taking cottages away from people, leaving them homeless. Does he?"

She reached in her pocket for her handkerchief and wiped her eyes and next her glasses. "In this case, I'm afraid it's really happening. We've lost our cottage. *I've* lost our cottage. It's all my fault. I've failed the both of us."

Hearing her say those words out loud knocked the wind out of me.

As I wandered around the cottage, it occurred to me that the things I held most dear to my heart weren't my hairbrushes, favorite boots, or the white fur pelt I'd been sleeping under since I was a baby. They were the lopsided candles that lit the living room at night; the rag rug that was so worn, patches of it felt like clouds on my bare feet; the tin cups from which we drank cider together, especially during Wolfstime; and the sofa that over the years had molded perfectly to our bodies, mine on the right, Granny's on the left.

I never thought I'd be forced to say good-bye to my home forever. Being able to come home to that little cottage—even after I ventured out to discover new places, and even if I decided someday to live in another house with my own husband and children—had always been a key part of my happy ending. It was the house Grandpa and Granny's brothers built for her. It was the place where my mother grew up and my parents got married. My mother gave birth to me right by the fireplace.

What would my mother do if she were still alive?

Finally, I returned to the kitchen. "Where are we going to go, Granny? Where are we going to live?" We had no other family to turn to.

"I truly don't know, child." She dabbed her eyes again and then blew her nose. Once I helped her to her feet, she began digging in the cabinets for bowls and pans as if someone were pulling her invisible strings, forcing her to bake when her aching body and battered soul weren't on board.

I couldn't bear to see my grandmother that way. I blinked back my tears and caressed my golden cross pendant. Suddenly, I had an idea. It was a long shot, but maybe if I could stop the tax man before he made it back to the royal castle . . .

Seventeen

I ran down the path and up the road as fast as I could, tracking Mr. Worthington's boot prints until they faded into the cobblestones of Main Street.

I paused to catch my breath, brushed my hair off my face, and took a look around, hoping to catch sight of the feathered cap bobbing among the villagers. Instead, I spotted on the road a splatted rotten tomato, and another just past it, in the unmistakable stamp of a very large boot. Behind a cart, a gang of little boys snickered mischievously, congratulating one another. "You pegged him right in that stupid hat o' his!" one said, validating my suspicion that the prints belonged to the tax man.

The red smears led to the tavern. I clenched my jaw as I imagined him in there, treating himself to a celebratory drink at having seized Granny's cottage in the king's name. Taking a deep breath, I stepped over a napping dog and pushed open the rusty double doors. I lowered my hood. It took a moment for my eyes to adjust to the dimness and for my nose to adjust to the stink of booze and sweat.

Beside an old dusty piano, a skinny woman thumped a tambourine while a man with a big mustache fiddled. A flaxen-haired girl in her mid-twenties suddenly lodged herself between me and my view of the room. "Can I help you, miss?" she asked over the din of music and bantering.

I regarded the tavern girl's tangled tresses, rosy lips, and light, piercing eyes. She wore a striped skirt that covered her legs, but her blouse showed off her freckled bosom and shoulders. She had a spark of confidence about her, like she knew her true self and no one could try to convince her otherwise. I gave her a small smile, realizing that if Granny saw me as a tavern girl, maybe it wouldn't be the most horrible fate in the land.

"O'er here, Gretchen!" a round, balding man from a crowded corner table hollered. "Bring me an' my chums anoth'r round. Come on, now. We haven't got all day."

One of his tablemates said, "What the dickens are ya talkin' 'bout? We most definitely have all day, and all tomorrow, and the day after . . ." and the table full of merry men chortled and clanked mugs.

The girl pressed her full lips together, and I had the distinct feeling that she and I were sharing a private girl-bonding moment. "Hold yer horses, gents," she called over her shoulder in a voice much gruffer than the one she'd used with me. Then she wove her way to the back of the tavern, which is where I spotted the feathered hat. Bellied up to the bar, Hershel Worthington was chugging an ale and talking to the aged bartender.

Pulling back my shoulders and raising my chin, I walked straight for the tax man. However, the closer I got, the more unsettled my stomach felt, and I had no choice but to backtrack a few steps and seek refuge behind a large knotty post. I took a big breath, and then another; and yet, my heart still raced. *You can do this, Red.*

Slumping forward, Mr. Worthington put his elbows on the bar. As he spoke to the older man, his voice carried over the music: "I wanted to have a son someday, but I married my dear Ernestine over a year ago, and suffice it to say, she wants nothing to do with me."

The bartender leaned over and took a whiff of him. "You don't smell too bad," he remarked. "And I'm thinkin' you make pretty good money, working for the king and all . . ." While he paused, he scratched his hoary head. "Oh! Have you tried being romantic with her? That seems to do the trick."

"Romantic, eh? Can't say I've tried that yet," Mr. Worthington said, before tilting the stein to his mouth.

The bartender grinned widely, revealing more gaps than teeth. "Works like magic, you'll see."

Suddenly, Gretchen loomed beside me. "Don't just stand there, honey," the tavern girl said with a wink. "Go an' sit by him, and ask him to buy you a drink."

I laughed nervously and waved my hands. "Oh, no. You have it all wrong. I just wanted to talk to him, that's all. Businesslike."

She set her tray down on the nearest table and fixed my hair, bringing the front portions over my shoulders. Next she pinched my cheeks. Her light blue eyes gleaming, she gave me the nod. "Go talk business."

I nodded back, amazed how she'd been able to restore my confidence. Before I lost it again, I walked up to the tax man and cleared my throat. "Mr. Worthington, may I have a word with you?"

"Always a pleasure, Miss Lucas," Mr. Worthington said, giving me no more than a sidelong glance. "Here to drink away your woes?"

"What can I get you, miss?" the bartender asked, drying his liver-spotted hands on a towel.

"I'm not thirsty," I told the old man, and he backed away, leaving the two of us to talk. "I'm here to make our woes disappear." I took the scroll Mr. Worthington had served Granny out of my pocket and placed it on the bar. "And you're going to help me."

"Is that so?"

"I'm here to pay my granny's debt."

"I see. I'm sorry to say, it's too late. However, I am a little bit curious. How exactly were you planning to do it?" He swung his legs around and faced me square on.

My heart pounded as my finger skimmed the gold cross resting on my collarbone. Drawing a deep, slow breath, I draped my hair over my left shoulder. His eyes followed my every move, even when he raised his stein to his lips for a quick swig. As he set his ale back down, I unclasped my necklace with a flick of my wrist.

"It was my mother's," I said, placing the cross pendant in his clammy, dirty palm.

"You don't say . . ." he said, though it was obvious he didn't care about sentimentalities. He was too busy biting down on it, to test if it was real gold.

December, three and a half years ago

I woke up with a start, unsure how I'd ended up under my bed. A fortress of pillows and covers encircled me, and though it was the coldest time of year, my hair was drenched with sweat.

I should have gotten up, but I felt unsettled—scared for a reason I couldn't put my finger on. So I stayed there until the rooster crowed, finally rolling out from under the bed once the little cottage filled with the noises of my granny banging around in the kitchen, commencing her morning routine. I stretched my arms over my head and rolled the kink out of my neck, trying to recall the dream I'd had. I was just bending to gather the pillows I'd stuffed beneath the bed when I spotted something twinkling between the floorboards. At first glance, it appeared to be a little golden star. But when I eased it up and out with my fingertips, I saw that it was a cross.

My heart leapt in my chest as I examined it in the early morning sunlight. It looked to be made of pure gold, and I loved how smooth it felt on the pads of my pointer finger and thumb. A tiny hole pierced through the top of it; it was meant to be a pendant.

I about jumped out of my skin when Granny charged into my room like a bull. "Daylight is burning, child. Get up and get me some eggs."

I tried to hide my newfound treasure from her but failed.

"Where did you find that?" she asked, crossing my room and staring at my palm like I was holding a poison apple.

"Under the bed."

Nodding slowly, her eyes glistened with apparent recognition. "It was your mother's."

"Did you give it to her, Granny?"

She shook her head. "I never knew where she got it. She wouldn't tell me. Said it was a secret. Here, hand it over," she said, gesturing for it. With a heavy heart, I surrendered it. Then she took me by the shoulders and turned me around, which was just as well because I didn't want her to see my scowl. Why did my granny have to be such a spoilsport all the time?

I felt her touch along the neckline of my nightdress. "Go see," she said, gently steering me to the looking glass above my bureau. Granny had threaded my mother's cross pendant onto her own necklace and fastened it around my neck. It was beautiful.

"She wanted you to have it," Granny said.

"Really?"

"Yes, I'm quite certain."

When I placed my hand over the cross for the very first time, I felt a wonderful warmth in my heart. "I will wear it always," I vowed.

I swallowed the bile in my throat. "So, do we have a deal, Mr. Worthington?" I asked, attempting to look directly into his shifty eyes. "Do I have your word that Granny and I can keep our cottage?"

"What would His Royal Highness want with a wee bit of gold when he has more treasure than anyone in the kingdom?" he asked, sliding my necklace along the bar and leaving it in front of me.

"What would the king want with a small, modest cottage in the woods, when he has the most exquisite castle in the kingdom—perhaps the entire land?" I countered.

"Everyone in the village must pay taxes to the king," he said, attempting to flag down the bartender. "Your grandmother failed to pay hers. So now we must take something from her. This is the way the kingdom works, missy."

"I realize that." I sighed. I didn't know what else to do, except get down on my knees and beg. "Please, Mr. Worthington. If we lose our home, we will have nowhere to go. We have no family. And my granny is too old to carry out her remaining days—I don't know, in a shack in the woods?" I'd just barely found out about losing the cottage, and the full repercussions hadn't hit me until then. Not only would we be homeless, Granny would have nowhere to bake. If she couldn't keep her business going, how would we ever make ends meet? I had to get the tax man to let Granny off the hook; it was our only hope! I beseeched him with my eyes, my heart, with every part of me. "This golden cross is all I have. It might not look all that impressive to you, but—"

He held his hand up and gestured for me to stop talking. While the indignity of having been shushed heated my cheeks, he called, "Willie! Fill me up," out of the corner of his mustached mouth.

The bartender waddled over to us, whistling to the music as he topped off Mr. Worthington's ale. I envied the old man, who didn't seem to have a care in the world.

"I'm afraid it's not enough," Mr. Worthington said, shaking his head.

Willie stopped whistling. "It's all that'll fit in the stein," he said apologetically, "but I'll bring you another if you need."

"I wasn't talking to *you*," Mr. Worthington snapped, and Willie slunk away in time to the music.

I opened my hands—I hadn't even noticed until then that I'd had them clenched into fists—and picked up the necklace. "It's enchanted," I blurted.

"Oh?" He stroked his long black beard as I dangled the pendant before his eyes. "How do you mean, enchanted?" He reached out, but I swayed the necklace just out of his reach.

Leaning closer to him, I whispered, "It's *magic*, Mr. Worthington. Whoever wears it will be under its spell. Its *love* spell." I knew I had to make the lie convincing. "The king might have more gold than he knows what to do with, but he's a widower, is he not? All he has to do is give this lovely necklace to a lady he desires, and she will adore him with all her heart."

"But the king doesn't need a love spell," Mr. Worthington said. "What he needs is a broom to keep all the women away from him."

"Yes, you're probably right." I sighed. "Well, you can't blame a girl for trying to save her granny's cottage, now can you?"

Mr. Worthington took a gulp out of his stein, only to peer into it, clearly surprised that it was already empty. "Miss Lucas, do you give me your word that this trinket is enchanted?" he asked.

My breath caught in my throat. Was my plan working? Perhaps the tax man was having a change of heart. "Yes. The wizard himself told me it was," I said, glad to finally be saying the truth.

He downed the rest of his ale then reached for the scroll. "Willie, bring me a bottle of ink, will you?" he called. A moment later, Willie dropped off the ink and then slowly scooted back to his customers at the far end of the bar.

With a faraway look in his eyes, Mr. Worthington took his feather out of his hat and wrote three of the most beautiful words across the parchment: PAID IN FULL. "I will hold off from reporting your grandmother to the king; however, next spring I shan't be as generous."

"I understand. Thank you," I said as I held my cross necklace for the last time. It was the most bittersweet feeling I'd ever had. On one hand, I wanted to dance around the tavern, laughing and perhaps even singing about having saved our cottage. On the other, parting with the cross pendant my mother wore made my throat close up and my eyes sting. I blinked hard and told myself that it was the right thing to do. The only thing to do. The instant I dropped the necklace into Mr. Worthington's hands—this time, for good—someone said my name.

"Red! What are you doing?"

I spun around to see Peter, his arms crossed over his chest and his eyes narrowed distrustfully at Mr. Worthington. "Peter, wh-what are you doing here?" I asked. I hated how I'd left things with Peter, but now was not the time to apologize and try to make things right between us. The ink hadn't even dried on the agreement. I just needed a few more minutes with Mr. Worthington, alone.

"I've come to check in on you, and it looks like it's a good thing I did." Though I hadn't seen Peter blink or move even a muscle, he seemed to have shot up ten inches. Mr. Worthington, on the contrary, shrunk away from him.

"Don't worry, Peter. Everything is fine, honestly," I said, forcing myself to smile up at him. Afraid he might do or say something to ruin my deal with the tax man, I quickly stood and gathered the scroll, placing it back inside my cloak.

I said, "So long, Mr. Worthington," and poked his feather back into his hat for him. Then, grabbing Peter's hand, I started dragging him toward the door.

"What was that all about, Red?" Peter asked. He dug in his heels, bringing us to an abrupt stop by the piano. "Why did you give him your cross?"

"Please, let's just get out of here. Then I'll tell you everything, I promise."

Tilting his head, he searched my face. A few seconds later, he lowered his eyebrows and said, "All right, but I'm holding you to that promise. No more secrets." Placing his hand on the small of my back, Peter guided me out of the tavern.

"How did you know I was in here, anyway?" I asked as he opened the door.

"My brothers said you'd walked by them. They said you looked upset, so they held back on pegging you with rotten vegetables."

"They're such little dears."

Just outside, we heard a little whimper. At our feet, the mutt whined and twitched in her sleep. The poor thing must've been having quite a nightmare.

There were two more nights of Wolfstime, and I wondered what my dreams would be like now. I already felt the emptiness where the cross used to lie against my chest. I reminded myself that I'd survived before without the pendant, when I'd lost it at the swimming hole. But that was before I'd found out that the wizard put a spell on it for my mother. Without the pendant, would I ever understand my Wolfstime dreams? Would I ever discover my true self?

Peter reached into his knapsack and tossed a small hunk of bread to the dog, so it could have something to eat when it woke up. Then, as he leaned against a lamppost, I told him why I'd gone after the tax man. I thought the part about Granny not being able to pay her taxes would be too mortifying to share, but Peter nodded understandingly, compassionately even. I knew I could trust Peter not to tell anyone.

"What you did was very heroic—and the bit about the pendant being enchanted with a love spell was particularly inspired." He shook his head and grinned. I couldn't help smiling as well. I *had* spun a dandy tale, and like the best stories, it had begun with a seed of truth. "But I know how much your mother's cross means to you," he said, much more somberly. "There has to be another way. I'll help you figure something out."

"Thank you, Peter, but it's all right. What's done is done. Besides, I'm sure my mother would have wanted it this way." Though I put on a brave face for him, I truly wanted to cry. We started walking down Main Street, and as we passed the alleyway where we'd danced earlier that afternoon, I wished he would fold me into his arms and tell me over and over again that everything was going to be all right.

But first, I knew I needed to tell Peter what had happened at market. I swallowed, mentally going over how exactly I was going to word the confession. I figured the best way was to tell the whole truth, come what may. As I spoke, he listened in silence. His Adam's apple bobbed in his throat when I got to the stealing portion of my confession, and a dark shadow filled his eyes when I recounted the kiss part. "Do you hate me now?" I bit my lower lip while I waited for him to answer.

"I could never hate you, Red. Actually, I'm glad you finally told me," he said, and then gave me the hug I'd been yearning for.

Resting my head on his shoulder, I let out a long stream of air. "Me too." I couldn't believe how much better it felt to be honest with him. I pulled him closer and never wanted to let go, but the sun was going down, and Peter had a nice stew to share with his family before joining his father and the other men on the wolf hunt. The thought of him up against the deadly beasts made me want to open up even more. "Peter, I . . ."

When my words trailed off, he held me out at arm's

length. His dark brown eyes widened as he waited for me to finish. But I couldn't. I couldn't tell him how I truly felt about him. The thought of him standing before me with his mouth open, not knowing how to respond because he didn't want to hurt me, parched my mouth and sank my stomach. If he didn't feel the same way about me, I'd be standing there like a heartbroken fool. Instead, I said, "I just want you to be careful tonight."

After the slightest of hesitations, he let go of my shoulders and ran a hand through his hair. "You have nothing to worry about. We have the best hunters and weapons in the village. And we'll be in groups."

"But I do worry about you. I can't help it."

"To be honest, I kind of like knowing that you care."

I swallowed. *I do care about you, Peter. Very much.* "You'd better get home. You don't want to miss your family's big supper," I said, though I didn't really want him to go.

"All right. Well, I'll see you around."

I waved good-bye as he turned around and started jogging back toward his house, none the wiser that I loved him.

Eighteen

My grandmother sat rigidly on the corner chair in the kitchen, her apron skewed, staring dazedly at the stacks of food that covered every last inch of the counter-tops. Knowing her, the excess of baked goods was her last-ditch effort at saving the cottage. Either that, or baking herself into a frenzy was her way of coping.

"I have good news, Granny. We aren't going to lose our cottage after all!"

She blinked twice and then turned to me as if just realizing I was there. "What in the land are you talking about, child?"

"The debt is gone. We're in the clear, at least for now." I handed my grandmother the agreement. Her forehead furrowed as she adjusted her glasses and read the PAID IN FULL. "How?"

I loosened the cloak from my shoulders and touched my collarbone.

"Oh, Red. The cross."

"It's all right, Granny," I said, sitting next to her. "I know it was my mother's, but I know if she were here, she would have done the same thing."

Granny opened her mouth and then shut it with a sigh. I guessed she was trying to thank me; she'd never been good at that. Finally, she said, "You're right. She would have."

"All right then," I said with a nod, "you've obviously baked enough to feed the entire kingdom. Let me help you get this cleaned up."

Granny frowned. "Hang on just a minute. There's something I need to get off my chest."

"What is it?"

Taking a deep, ragged breath, she wrung her hands. "Listen, Red. I . . . I'm sorry I said those things earlier today."

I bit my lower lip and tried not to look shocked as she studied my face. If she hardly ever thanked anyone, she even more seldom apologized. "I'm also sorry I brought your mother into it. It's just that, I blame myself for what happened to Anita. I wanted to protect her, but I failed."

"I'm sure you did everything you could," I said.

"Not everything, I'm afraid."

"It's not your fault my parents went out in the woods and a hunter accidentally shot them."

"I'm not just talking about that," she said. "You're a lot like your mother, you know." She brushed my cheek with her fingertips and then promptly returned her hand to her lap. "She had a wild side, you might say." For a brief instant, her lips formed a small smile. "Sometimes, I sense that wild side in you, too, and to be honest, it scares the dickens out of me. That's why I got you the hood. But that won't protect you from everything. It won't protect you from getting your heart broken."

"Granny, what are you trying to say?"

"You see, I tried to spare you what really happened that night when your parents died."

I leaned forward, wanting—and yet more than a bit nervous—to hear what had really happened. "You lied to me?"

She shifted in her chair. "I didn't lie, not really. I just left some things out." She exhaled loudly, making her cheeks puff out. "That tragic night, before they ran into the woods, they'd had a terrible fight. I came running into their room—your room now, as you know—and tried to break it up. Your father didn't lay a hand on her, not that I saw anyway. But he did snap her necklace right off her neck, which infuriated your mother."

"If that happened the night they died, then I'm guessing it somehow ended up under the bed, where I found it?" I asked.

She nodded. "Yes, that's what I figured, too. Now, where was I? Oh, yes. Your parents had had quite a few fights before, but this one was different somehow. It had the weight of finality. One look at your mother's tearstained face, and I've never seen such anguish. I knew her heart had been broken. She tore off into the woods, and he followed her. I tried to stop them, but . . ."

"The hunters got to them first," I finished for her, and she nodded solemnly.

"You were only a baby, but somehow, you must have sensed that something tragic had happened to them. You cried the whole night, clear through to breakfast. I swore to you that come hell or high water, I'd keep you safe. You're all I've got, child."

I'd been so enraptured by Granny's story that I just then realized the sun was going down. Granny must have noticed at the same time, because after glancing out the window, she jumped up. "Well, enough chin-wag. It's almost dusk, and it looks like another spring shower's coming in, too. Go fetch the clothes off the line, and don't tarry."

The instant I stepped out the back door, a gale blew my hair into my eyes and inflated my cloak like the sails of a ship, making it tough to see and walk. But I made it to the clothesline and hurriedly began piling the linens in my basket, until something caught my eye and made my heart skip a beat: giant wolf tracks, in the soft dirt behind the old oak tree. They were fresh enough that

I guessed they'd been made last night. I followed them and gasped when I saw how they skirted the cottage and continued past the chicken coop, to the stream. Luckily, the wolf had left the chickens alone, but who was to say the fowl would survive tonight, or the night after, for that matter?

Leaving my chore unfinished, I hurried back inside. While Granny made the Wolfstime rounds in our bedrooms and the living room, I slipped into the kitchen to lock it down and start making the cider. The whole while, I couldn't stop thinking about the wolves. I'd always been deathly afraid of them; but now, I hated them.

I hated them for plaguing our village with horror an entire week of every month. I hated them for killing our neighbors' cow and sheep and our chickens. I hated them for killing my great-uncles and grandfather in cold blood. I hated how they killed them before my grandmother's terrified eyes—a living nightmare that compelled her to speak out against those who believed they could somehow defeat the monsters, or those who weren't sufficiently fearful of them—and how her fervor marked her as the laughingstock of the village, then as well as now. I hated them for putting my parents in death's way and forcing our menfolk into a seemingly everlasting and futile chase. I hated them for making me worry about Peter and his first night with the hunters and for leaving menacing tracks just outside our cottage walls.

How I would love to be the one to finally kill the wolves and save the village from their reign of terror!

As these thoughts built up inside of me, I scrubbed the bowls, pans, and spoons harder and harder. I rummaged under the sink for a dish towel, and that was when it came to me. Dogs loved my biscuits, and like Violet had said the night of the bonfire, a wolf was essentially an overgrown mongrel.

If I lace biscuits with rat poison and scatter them along the tracks the wolf left last night, perhaps I can be the one who finally kills the wolves!

I took out the rat poison that we kept under the sink and sprinkled it on the cookies, putting my plan in motion. I almost told Granny my idea, but when I spied her leaning against the living room wall and holding her aching arm, I felt like she was going through enough. "Looks like I left a few towels up on the line, Granny. I'll be right back in," I called. Then I slipped out the back door and scattered the poisoned dog biscuits alongside the wolf prints.

With the storm blowing in, the sky was darkening at a rapid rate, and yet the clouds could not contest the moon. Tipping back my head, I let the moon's light embrace me. Once I was back inside, I boarded up the back door, slowly breathing in and out. It was as if the moon's glow had somehow gotten inside of me, and I held on to the sensation as best I could as Granny and I wrapped up the final minutes of the day and I ducked into my room for the night.

I shed my clothes on the floor, hung my hood on the bedpost, and flopped onto my bed. Gazing at the shapes the candlelight created on the canopy, I felt a sudden rush of feverish heat. If Granny happened to stick her head in to check on me, she would come unglued—not only since I hadn't bothered to put on a nightgown, but because I'd unlocked and wedged open my shutters, just to get some fresh, cool air.

Standing before the window in my undergarments, with the glow of candles behind me and the vast dangers of Wolfstime in front of me, I felt an odd mixture of power and vulnerability. Although I knew I should lock my room back up and get into bed, I found myself pondering Peter's whereabouts at that very moment. Had the hunters, armed with torches, weapons, and a sense of invincibility, marched through the park and into the graveyard? Had they gathered in the village center or at the schoolhouse? Or had they trooped straight down Main Street and into the forest?

I leaned closer to the open window, wondering if they would come within view of our cottage. Clouds veiled the enormous moon like puffs of silvery-gray gauze. The wind stirred the leaves, and squirrels chattered off and on in the trees. There were no hunters, though.

With a little imagination, I was able to trick myself into seeing them pass by the cottage—all but Peter, who spied me standing in my window wearing next to nothing. In my mind, he stopped in the shadows while the other hunters carried on without him. I wasn't sure what to do next, because he didn't realize I knew he was there, and I didn't want this little game to end quite yet. So I began brushing my hair for him. I took special care in each and every stroke, starting at the root and running the bristles seamlessly to the ends. The wind entered my room, caressing my face, neck, and shoulders. Peter stepped out from the shadows into the luminous moonlight, and I drank in the approval and appreciation written all over his handsome face.

I wasn't sure exactly when the rain had begun but, suddenly, raindrops were coming into my bedroom. Blinking, I closed and locked the window. I tried to keep the best parts of my fantasy about Peter alive as I fluffed my pillow and slipped into bed. But then, as I was wont to touch my neck as I drifted off to sleep, the pendant's absence made me start. It would be my first slumber in over three years without my mother's cross—and not only that, but it would be my first night knowing it to be enchanted.

If I hadn't made the deal with the tax man—if I still wore the necklace—would my Wolfstime dreams become increasingly extreme, as the wizard had cautioned my mother? He'd told me that my mother longed to understand the meaning of her dreams, because she'd been so desperate to discover her true self. But as for me, what if I was too afraid to find my true self?

What if I just wanted to fall asleep peacefully instead of fearfully and have dreams like everybody else had?

What if I wanted to dream about Peter?

Friday, May 18

I sat straight up in my bed. Clutching my pillow to my chest, I rocked back and forth. My eyes prickled and my body felt as if it had been tied to the vane of a windmill for days on end.

What had I dreamed to make me feel so battered?

I rocked some more, blinking back tears I didn't understand.

It finally dawned on me that the sun had risen—and yet the rooster hadn't crowed. *Everything is fine*, I consoled myself as I swapped my nightdress for skirt and blouse, topped it all off with my cloak, and fetched the egg basket. The instant I stepped into the backyard, the air took on a sinister chill. And it was quiet, too quiet. *Something is wrong.*

"Granny! Come quick!"

Huge wolf tracks had torn up the tender springtime soil in the same pattern I'd dropped the poisoned dog biscuits—with a detour directed straight to the chicken coop.

My grandmother appeared on the back porch, rubbing her hands on her apron. "No. *No*, not again." She bustled across the clearing, trying to stop me from going in. But she was too late. As I stepped through the door, the light of day flooded the coop. I shook uncontrollably as four deep gashes—no doubt the claw-marks of the wolf—loomed on the wall before me.

Ripping the broomstick off its hook, I started sweeping up the bloody feathers and bird parts. The gore clumped and streaked, and though all I accomplished was smearing it about even worse, I kept sweeping. "With any luck, our chickens will be that wolf's final meal," I said.

"Don't be ridiculous, child. This was merely an appetizer." Granny waved her hands around as if I hadn't even noticed the massacre.

"I poisoned the dog biscuits and scattered them outside the cottage last night, in case the wolf dared come back here. In case it went after our chickens again."

"You did *what*?" she asked.

"The biscuits are gone, Granny." I smiled, feeling oddly serene despite the morbid sight, stench, and stillness surrounding us. "Maybe the wolf is dead."

"Haven't you heard a single thing I've told you, all these years? This is no ordinary wolf, child. It's more powerful than you can ever imagine." Granny snatched the broom from my grasp. In one hand she held the broomstick, and in the other, my shoulder, as she marched me out of the coop. Next she set the bottom of the broom on one of the wolf tracks. The paw print eclipsed the bristles, and its claws splayed out even farther. I knew the wolf was gigantic—I'd seen its tracks before—but I couldn't help gasping. Granny nodded. "You see? A poisoned dog biscuit won't give this creature a bellyache, let alone kill it."

"The hunters went out last night, you know," I said, my stomach twisting as I thought of Peter. "I just wanted to help."

Granny nodded and handed me back the broom. "Let's pray the monster stuck with a poultry diet," she said as she walked back into the house.

I finished washing up the chicken coop and then returned to my room for my bow and arrows. Even though Granny thought it impossible, I wanted to hold on to the belief that somewhere out there was a dead—or at least, very sick—wolf. And luckily, tracking was what I did best.

As I hiked, I daydreamed about discovering the wolf's dead body in the forest. No one knew for sure how many wolves roamed the woods and terrorized the village, but if the poisoned dog biscuits vanquished one, I could make more and eventually do them all in.

I would be the village hero! The very thought of it made me grin ear to ear. Word would spread near and far, and everybody would respect me and love me.

Like earlier that morning, the air grew colder, lending it a certain bite. My heart hammered—and not merely with exertion—when the paw prints led me to the hill behind the blacksmith's shop. I took a deep breath and shivered. Had a wolf wreaked havoc at Peter's place last night?

Drawing my bow, I followed the tracks to a grove of towering evergreens. When I spotted blood on the ground, I hoped it was from a rabbit, or perhaps a deer.

But it wasn't. It was from a man.

Nineteen

I just stood there, paralyzed, not knowing what to do. Taking in the torn-apart neck, shoulder, and thigh—the blood-drenched shirt, and legs bent at ungainly angles—I wasn't sure if I screamed out loud, or if it was only in my mind.

Finally, I mustered up enough courage to move my wobbly legs closer. It was Amos Slade, the hunter. I would recognize that shaggy hair and bushy gray mustache anywhere. Peter and his father had been out with Amos last night, and my stomach roiled with worry. "Oh, no. No, no. Please let the others be safe," I prayed in a choked-up whisper.

I swallowed back the sour taste of vomit and dropped to my knees beside Amos Slade. With trembling hands, I felt for a breath. It just seemed like the thing to do; but really, all I had to do was look into the old man's cloudy eyes to know for certain that he was gone. "Oh, Amos," I said as I closed his eyelids.

The instant I touched him, I saw hundreds of glowing, razor-sharp teeth, coming straight for me. Terror snapped itself around my neck like a bear trap, and I couldn't breathe. The world went black, as if a dark curse had blocked the sun.

The next thing I knew, someone was gently shaking me.

"Red? Red, answer me. Are you all right?"

Peter.

Peter!

I pried open my eyes. Peter's handsome face, illuminated by sunlight, came into a fuzzy focus. "Peter, is that really you?" Suddenly, pain thudded on the back of my head like I'd been walloped with a croquet mallet, and I grimaced.

He was kneeling before me, his hands on my shoulders and his brown eyes wide. "Yes, it's me." He wrapped me in a huge, warm hug and whispered into my hood, "You scared the dickens out of me, Red! What happened? Are you all right?"

"I'm fine, Peter." He let go of me and we both scrambled to our feet. "I think I just must have hit my head somehow . . ." After I'd closed Amos Slade's eyes, I must have rocked backwards; and though the tree had broken my fall, it had also given me a big knot on the back of my head. "I'm fine," I repeated, mainly for myself. "I only wish I could say the same for poor Mr. Slade."

Then I recalled the horrific vision I'd had when I'd touched Amos, and my heart raced. I couldn't get the frightful image of lethal, glowing teeth and the undeniable sense of terror out of my mind. It was almost as if I'd somehow been let in to experience what Amos had gone through in his last living moments. That made no sense, though. Maybe something like that could happen if I was a witch or a sorcerer, but that was just crazy. In all likelihood, the vision was just my imagination getting the better of me. Then again, perhaps I'd hit my head and fallen asleep just long enough to have one of my Wolfstime dreams.

I heard the snap-crackle of pinecones underfoot, and reached for my quiver. "Who's there?" I called.

Peter jogged over to a bush and waved my weapon down. "Look here. It's just Amos's hound." The pitiful dog must have been hiding there. Had he seen the wolf murder his owner? "Poor thing," Peter said, trying to get him to come. The dog seemed dazed; yet when he caught a whiff of something, he snarled and backed away. After a moment, he took off for the woods.

Peter shook his head and sighed as he approached Amos's corpse. "He insisted on hunting the wolves after the rest of us had given up and headed home for the night. Papa and I tried to talk some sense into him. Lot of good it did . . . Stubborn old bastard." His voice hitched, like he was trying to hold back a sob.

As for me, I couldn't hold back. I wept, and again, Peter embraced me.

"Oh, Peter, I hate this. I want to leave. I want to

go far, far away from this place," I said between sniffs. "Someplace where horrible monsters don't lurk in the shadows."

"I'll take you wherever you want to go, Red," Peter said, steering me down the hill, away from the grisly scene.

I dug in my heels, making him come to an abrupt stop. "Really, Peter? You want to come with me?"

"Sure, why not?"

I sniffled a little. "Do you promise?"

"I promise," he said, looking me directly in the eyes. Not for the first time, I wondered what he saw when he gazed at me like that. But this time, I wanted to help him discover the possibility of *us*.

Having found Amos Slade dead in the forest would no doubt horrify and sadden me for the rest of my life. However, it also made me realize just how short life was—how precious every moment was. It very well could have been Peter lying on the ground, torn to shreds. It could have been me. Maybe I didn't have all the time in the world to show Peter how I felt.

Without another thought, I rose onto my toes and

leaned in to him. My eyes closed, and my lips found his. At first, our lips barely grazed, soft as feathers in a breeze, and I drank in the sweet air that had been inside of him only a second prior. I pressed my body against his and pulled him closer by the back of his neck. He removed my hood and his fingers ran through the waves of my hair. As our kiss deepened, we took turns exploring each other's lips, mouths, necks. It felt so nice and familiar and yet, at the same time, so deliciously dangerous.

I completely lost track of time, caring about nothing but Peter as he answered my unspoken questions. He centered a gentle kiss on my parted lips, and I opened my eyes to see him smiling at me. I was thankful when his hands snaked around my waist because I felt quite certain my knees would give out at any moment.

"Thank you, Peter," I said, still feeling a bit woozy.

"For what?"

"For giving me a second chance at a first kiss."

I wished I could live in the afterglow of having kissed Peter forever—or at least a little longer. However, as I stepped into the kitchen, it was obvious I'd need twice as much time as usual to deliver all those baked goods. And I'd really have to rush if I was to make my noon-time date with the talking crow. As I let go of the bliss of kissing Peter, the grief of Amos Slade's gruesome death began to pour back in, and I felt a lump forming in my throat.

"Where have you been all morning?" Granny asked, and then shook her head. "Never mind, forget I asked. We have much to do, and I'm too exhausted to deal with your capers today." She turned back toward the sink.

"I followed the wolf tracks," I confessed.

She stopped rinsing her coffee cup and whirled around.

"I told you that would never work."

"I had to see if I'd poisoned it."

"You disobeyed me."

"I don't know if the wolf is dead, Granny. I never

found it. But . . ." There was no gentle way to break the news. She'd learn soon enough, anyway. I lowered my hood. "Amos Slade . . ."

"What of him? Is he harassing you for peach pie again? Land sakes, that fool just doesn't get it, does he? How can I make him a fresh peach pie when the peaches aren't ready to be picked? It's like living in that dirty old shack day in and day out, with no one but a hound to talk to, is drying up his brain. Soon there'll be nothing but a crusty little raisin rattling around his skull, and I'll be damned if he still asks for peach pie!"

"He's dead, Granny. Wolf tracks all around. He's . . . not going to be asking for peach pie, ever again."

She blinked. "Oh."

Her face went as pasty as flour, and I feared she might topple over, so I scooted the rush-topped stool to her.

Lowering herself, she stared out the window. She took off her glasses and rubbed them clean on her apron. It must have been a trick of the sunlight pouring into the kitchen and onto her face, but I thought I might have caught a cursory glimpse of a younger Widow Lucas in her.

June, ten years ago

I peeked through the curtain to see our neighbor, Mr. Slade, waiting at the front door. He had a mop of brownish-gray hair on his head and a smaller one under his nose, and blue-gray eyes that somehow managed to look grumpy and kind at once. In one hand, he held his floppy brown hat, and in the other, a bouquet of wildflowers.

"Granny! Mr. Slade's here," I said, running into the kitchen to fetch her. "Looks like he's selling flowers again."

Granny had been baking peach pies when he'd rapped on the door, and now she had a dusting of flour on her cheek. She wagged her finger at me. "Don't open the door until he's gone away. Do you hear me, child?"

I watched him finally walk down the pathway with his hat on his head and his shoulders slumped. He looked so sad; I couldn't stand it. I'd found a halfpenny on the street in the village and was saving it for something special. Maybe that was enough for one of his flowers, and it would make him happy.

But by the time I'd run to my bedroom and back down onto the porch, he was gone. Anyway, I didn't need to buy a flower because he'd left the entire bouquet by the door. When I gave the flowers to Granny, she waved her hand at them like they were useless, but I thought I'd spotted something in her eyes that day. Something that looked an awful lot like a sparkle.

"Amos Slade fancied you, didn't he?" I asked, astounded that it had taken me so long to piece it all together. Someone having those kinds of feelings for my grandmother was more than a bit awkward to imagine. Naturally, I could imagine my grandparents being sweethearts, long, long ago. But my grandpa died before I was born; so in my eyes, he was more of an idea than a living, breathing man. On the contrary, I knew Amos Slade. And, up until an hour ago, Amos had been a living, breathing man.

Granny's shoulders were shaking, almost as if she was sobbing—or trying like crazy not to. Maybe my grandmother had felt something for Amos, as well. "Wait, did you two have a secret romance?" I asked.

Granny blinked a few times and slowly put her glasses back on. "Nonsense. I don't know what you're yakking about, child." She stood and finished packing the baskets. After filling me in on the day's deliveries and telling me to put in an order for some new chickens with Farmer Thompson, she said softly, "Amos didn't deserve to die that way. It's a shame. A waste." She clenched her hands into fists. "I wish your poison had killed the wolf." She handed me one of the baskets. "You'd better get a wiggle on," she said. "And don't forget your hood."

Shortly thereafter, I tore off up the road, loaded down with two baskets and my bow and arrows. As I headed toward the gully where the bilberries grew, I stopped at the customers' houses along the way, dropping off their baked goods and dog biscuits, collecting their payments, and, when I arrived at the Thompsons' house, putting in an order for more chickens.

When I made it to the gully, I splashed my face with springwater and sat to rest on a log. I held a crumpet and whistled. "Come out, come out, wherever you are!" No crows—let alone talking ones—appeared. "Heathcliff? Please come out. I have a nice tasty crumpet for you. I'm here to see the wizard. He's expecting me."

"Give it."

Startled, I dropped the crumpet into the spring and cursed under my breath. In the entrance to the cave, the bird tilted its scruffy black-feathered head. "Don't worry, I have another. Here," I said, holding a crumpet in the air. He circled around my head twice and then grabbed it in his pointy beak. He flew back to the cave and began taking his good sweet time picking at the bread.

"Will you take me to see Knubbin now?" I rose and gathered my baskets.

The bird blinked its beady eyes, and with crumbs falling out of his beak, said, "No."

"Stop playing games with me, Heathcliff. It's past noon, and you're making me even later."

"No one is home."

"Oh." Panic seeped into my gut. I'd been worried about finding the crow in the first place, and even more nervous to discover whether or not the wizard made good on his promise. "All right, then. When do you expect him back?"

The crow blinked. "Nevermore."

"Will you take me to his place?" Perhaps Heathcliff was wrong. I'd come this far, and I'd feel a lot better seeing whether or not the wizard was home for myself. "Here, I have another delicious crumpet. And a raisin cookie, if that's to your liking."

The bird swooped down for the treats. I waited as patiently as possible for him to finish eating and, finally, we were on our way.

The instant I spotted the rickety cabin, I knew something was amiss. The garden was picked-over, the windows closed, and the mare missing. The place appeared to be deserted. My heart sunk when I knocked and he didn't answer. Just to be sure that he wasn't there, I set my baskets down on the little porch and let myself in.

"Is anyone home? Knubbin? Are you here?" I asked, leaving the door cracked open as I wandered in. A pot crashed to the floor and I must have jumped twice my height. I hoped it was the wizard, but when I saw that it was just the gray cat, chasing spiders in the rafters, I exhaled with disappointment.

While the pans and miniature furnishings were still there, the wizard's animal figurines, moon and stars painting, black cloak, and jugs of mead were missing. Clearly, Knubbin hadn't merely gone on a walk. He had

packed his personal belongings—and my life savings—
and hightailed it on his horse. Where he'd gone, I had no
idea. *How could he have betrayed me like this?*

My eyes burning, I took one last glance around, and
that was when I saw it. "I could've sworn this wasn't here
just a second ago," I said out loud. On the curio where
the wizard's figurines once sat was an amber-hued jar the
size of a thimble. The note tucked behind the jar read:
RUB SALVE ON, FEEL NOT THE PAIN in bilberry ink. Was this
the magic salve?

A voice came from behind me: "Aha!"

It startled me so badly I jumped. And when I whirled
around, I had to blink to make sure it was indeed the
wizard who was looming in the entryway. He wore his
long black cloak and pointy-toed boots, and he appeared
to have bathed and trimmed his beard. As he crossed the
room toward me, I wondered why he was so much more
put-together than yesterday.

"You've found it," he said, lifting the jar off the shelf.
When he handed it to me, he gave it a jiggle. The jar lit

up, like a firefly was trapped inside. It sparkled brilliantly, and I had the wonderful sensation that the magic in this tiny bottle would change Granny's life forever.

I couldn't wait to give it to her. And since this was the last night of Wolfstime, she'd never have to live with the pain, ever again. I beamed at the wizard. "Thank you so much, Knubbin. I thought you'd forgotten."

"Well, isn't that a coincidence? I thought you had forgotten to come for it," Knubbin said. "But then I forgot that I ever thought that, and so here I am. However, I cannot stay but a minute or six, you see, because I must put the finishing touches on my relocation spell." His beady eyes shifted hither and thither, and had I not known better, I would have said the wizard was nervous. "They are on their way."

"Who?" I asked.

"It does not concern you as it does me, so never mind that, and instead look there." He pointed at my hand, and I saw that the jar had stopped glowing.

I shook it as Knubbin had, but nothing happened. "Is something wrong with it?" I asked.

"There's one teensy-tiny ingredient the spell is missing, one you'll need to add in order for it to work," he said. "The one who loves your grandmother most of all must see it to its completion, you see. But don't fret, poppet. You're a smart girl, and I know you'll accomplish the quest with no hitches whatsoever."

"A quest? But I've never even journeyed to another village," I said.

"You told me you wanted to go off into the world and have adventures," he said, grandly sweeping his hand before us. "You want to find your happy ending, isn't that right? Or has your plan changed in a mere day's time?"

"No, I *do* want to do that. I just . . ." My mind was spinning. I wasn't quite sure what was happening. *What game is the wizard playing with me?*

"And don't you want the magic salve so your poor grandmother can bake and knit and sleep without having to take poppy dust at night?" He wrinkled his long, narrow nose. "Terrible stuff, or so I hear."

"Well, yes, of course I want Granny's pain to be gone. That's why I came to you in the first place."

"Very good, very good indeed. Then it is settled. You shall leave the village to go on a quest for the final ingredient in the magic salve that will heal your grandmother. And although I cannot know for sure, I have a good feeling that you will experience an adventure or five along the way, and if everything works out, you will find your happy ending." The wizard clapped three times and gestured toward the door.

"Oh, one more thing." He flipped his hand palm-up, and like the gypsies at market who can make objects materialize seemingly out of thin air, his leather belt-pouch appeared. I heard the jingle of coins as he gave the pouch a little toss and dangled it by its drawstring. "You told me when you gave me this money that it was your future, did you not?"

I nodded.

"Now I'm giving it back to you, every last cent of it. I predict that you'll need your future more than I. Besides, it's always a good idea for common folk to bring money along on their quests. You never know when you'll need to pay a toll or buy something to eat."

I reached out for the pouch but then hesitated when his mouth curved into a yellow-toothed smirk. "But I thought all magic came with a price," I said slowly.

"It does, that's true. Not even I know what the future brings, but that's what makes life so interesting. Now, it's time for you to run along. Go, go, go."

"Wait, what is the ingredient I'm to find on this quest?" I asked.

"Ah, a good question. All you need is a drop of water from Lake Nostos. Just one little drop, no more, and no less—"

"Lake Nostos?" I wanted to laugh and cry at the same time.

The wizard arched his left eyebrow and tilted his head like an owl. "You look as if I've told you to go fetch a scale from a sleeping dragon. It's just a little lake water, what could be simpler?"

"Yes, but everybody knows that Lake Nostos isn't real. It's just a tale from a dusty old storybook."

He clasped his hands together. "You know the story, then?"

"Of course I know the story. My grandmother read it to me when I was a little girl. It was one of my favorites. But—"

"Oh good, good, good. You're halfway there."

"Knubbin, you're missing the point. It's just a fairy tale. It's not true. How can I find a lake that doesn't exist?" I clenched my jaw in frustration.

"In every tale is a nugget of truth—especially those found in dusty old storybooks. You have to open your heart and let the truth find you. Some say the truth rings as clear and sweet as a nightingale's song."

The crow swooped in through the door and perched on the curio. With his beak, he picked up the note and passed it to me, but since I was already holding the jar and the bag of coins, I had to juggle it awkwardly.

"Ah, yes, thank you, Heathcliff," Knubbin said, patting the bird on his feathered head. "Now, take our guest back to the gully. She has much to do before the birds fly south."

My head spun as I followed the bird and then made

my way down the road and back to the cottage. The wizard was right. For as long as I could remember, I'd wanted to leave the village and find my happy ending. But going on a quest to find an imaginary lake? That had never, ever been part of my plan.

Twenty

I flung open the cottage door and almost ran smack into Granny. "Mayor Filbert has called an emergency town meeting," she said, "and I need to be early so I can stand front and center. They've got some meaty issues on the table. Guess they've finally decided that the wolf pack is a bigger problem than they thought it was, now that they'll have to bury Amos Slade. Once again, it's up to me to be the voice of reason in a roomful of idiots," she said, clicking her tongue.

Normally, I'd cringe at the thought of Granny taking the stand. And given the reaction of the villagers to her at previous meetings—the sniggering, the pointing, the pitying shaking of heads—I might beg her to reconsider. Not that it would do a lick of good, but at least I could find a little peace in knowing that I'd tried.

But today, I said nothing to stop her. Granny had lived in the village all her life, so maybe she was right about the wolves being too powerful for the hunters to kill. If so, I didn't want Peter to be the next hunter to die at the claws and teeth of a wolf.

I helped her wrap her shawl over her bun and around her shoulders. In the process, I grabbed her right arm and lifted her sleeve. She forcefully pulled away, demanding to know what I thought I was doing, but not before I got a cursory glimpse of her mysterious scar. I saw four red, inflamed gashes. It was hideous, and looked like it was excruciatingly painful. My heart raced as I realized that it almost exactly matched the slash mark the wolf had made on the wall of the chicken coop.

"It's from the wolf, isn't it?" I asked. "The wolf hurt you, didn't it? And yet, you escaped it. How did you get away from it, Granny?"

"Don't be ridiculous. I'm going to be late. Get out of my way."

"I'm going with you." I ran to my room and placed the salve, note, and leather pouch full of coins into the wooden box in my bureau. Before closing the lid, I shook the tiny amber-colored jar. Nothing happened.

The villagers swarmed the town hall like bees around a hive. Miss Cates cornered Granny to chat about wedding cake ideas, but Granny quickly wrenched away to secure a spot in the front row. As I pushed my way through the crowd, two carrottopped children ran smack into my legs, making me trip. Thankfully, Priscilla was right behind them to steady me. "I'm so sorry, Red," she said, shaking her head. "Believe me, I'm already counting down the days till they're old enough to leave the nest." Baby Ezekiel cooed at me from his swaddle, and I smiled and tugged his ear.

Violet, Florence, and Beatrice held signs reading: DON'T LET THE BEAST TAKE OUR FORGET-ME-NOT BALL AWAY FROM US! and bounced around the building with a growing herd of devotees.

Priscilla arched her right eyebrow. "It's always something with them, isn't it?" Her twins twined around her legs, and the baby babbled adorably.

"Look, Ma! Doggie!" said the little girl twin, pointing at Amos Slade's hound. Sure enough, the dog was keeping a close eye on his new master, who made his way into the center of the bustling room with his father. My heart skipped a beat when Peter's handsome brown eyes found mine. He grinned and mouthed, *"Hallo."*

I gave him a little wave, until I realized that Priscilla was watching us with interest. "Looks like Peter has taken a shining to you, my dear," she said.

I felt heat rush to my face, and I let out a strange giggle. "Well, I don't know abou—"

She pressed her finger on my lips and lowered her eyebrows. "Yes, you *do*. I might not be a fortune-teller, but I know what true love looks like." She slid her finger down to my chin and angled my face back toward Peter, who was coming straight for me. However, Hershel Worthington had edged up to us, blocking my view. Priscilla's baby batted at the feather in his hat like a kitten.

"Ah, if it isn't the lovely Miss Lucas. May I have a quick word with you?" the tax man asked, and Priscilla gave him a curt nod and went after the twins, who looked to be headed for the fountain.

"I'm glad I bumped into you. I wanted to ask, is there something I need to do to activate the magic?" He reached in his belt-pouch and pulled out my mother's gold cross, holding it in front of my face. "I figured there must be some magic words?"

I never thought I'd see it again, and under these circumstances, it felt like a blow to my gut. I swallowed and tightly gripped the sides of my cloak. I wanted to reach out and grab it, but I knew I couldn't. A deal was a deal. "Just tell her how you feel about her. Those are the magic words."

Mr. Worthington raised his left eyebrow musingly. As he tucked the necklace back into his pouch, Peter sidled up to us. "Excuse me, Mr. Worthington," Peter said, clapping the older man on the back. "Mayor Filbert is asking for you. He's outside, in the back, getting a little fresh air before calling the meeting to order." Then Peter spun him around and walked several paces alongside him, saying, "Over this way. Yes, that's good. All right, good luck." Smiling, Peter jogged back to me.

"Since when have you been all chummy with the tax man?" I asked. "What was that about?"

Peter's smile broadened, and I lost myself in his dimple and the way his eyes sparkled. "I happen to know that my brothers have a bushel of rotten tomatoes, cabbages, and eggs to throw at the bastard. I was just getting him within range," he said.

I knew the thought of Hershel Worthington being pelted by stinking balls of slime should make me laugh, but I couldn't help feeling a little bad for the man. However, I did what I had to do, and what was the harm in having him believe that a beautiful gold pendant and a few tender words would make his wife fall in love with him? "You boys are just a bunch of bullies."

"I know. So, what're you doing here, anyway? I thought you hated town meetings."

"You'd hate them, too, if your grandmother got her jollies out of taking the stand and getting the whole village riled up. It's so embarrassing."

"Ah, well, she has good intentions. She just wants everybody to be safe from the wolves—especially you. And can you blame her? You're pretty nice to have around." He tucked a tendril of my hair behind my ear, and I swallowed hard. When he wrapped his long, muscular arms around me, I melted so deeply into his chest I heard the soft and steady patter of his heart.

Much too soon, he broke our embrace. Then again, a hundred years would've been too soon. "So, you never answered my question. What brings you to the meeting?" he asked. "And don't tell me it's to support your chum, the tax man, when he takes the stand in a couple of minutes."

"I think I might actually be here to support Granny."
My words surprised even myself.

Grinning, he rocked back on his heels. "The Lucas
women united. Now that's more than a bit daunting."

Florence's stepfather, Mayor Filbert, yelled, "Order,
order!" as he rang the bell. "I call to order this town
meeting. Our first order of business is the most unfortunate and untimely—though he was rather old, come to
think of it, and probably wouldn't have made it through
the winter—"

Florence's mother elbowed him and whispered
harshly, *"Benjamin."*

The mayor cleared his throat and straightened his
belt. "Back to topic, our first order of business is the
recent and tragic death of Amos Slade, may he rest in
peace."

"May he rest in peace," the townsfolk repeated.

"Yes, yes. Thank you for that. All right then," he continued, adjusting his glasses as he glanced down at a scroll.
"Upon study of the body and the tracks surrounding the

place of death, it is clear that Mr. Slade was attacked and killed by a very large wild animal."

"The wolves!" Seamstress Evans yelled. Her young son held up his wooden sword and grunted.

While other villagers joined in, the mayor cleared his throat. "People, quiet down. Quiet!" As soon as the din died down enough for him to carry on, he said, "Yes, the consensus is that the wolves are to blame for this horrific act. We have no way of knowing whether it's the same wolf that's been wreaking havoc on our farm animals or one that's particularly keen on human blood. What we *do* know is one of our finest hunters is dead."

"What the dickens are we going to do about it?" a middle-aged woman with a green shawl over her head demanded.

"These bloodthirsty beasts won't rest until they've slaughtered the lot of us," the shoemaker added.

"The wolves *will* attack again. We have no choice but to hunt down and kill the entire pack!" Peter's father said.

The mayor nodded at the blacksmith. "And the

sooner, the better. Any man, young or old, who's willing to fight in tonight's hunting party, gather by the fountain immediately following this meeting."

"You're all a bunch of idiots," Granny's voice called out from the front row. "Soon you'll be a bunch of *dead* idiots!"

"That's one of her favorite sayings," I whispered to Peter.

He nodded and then a second later said, "Stay right here, all right? I need to do something real quick."

"Everything all right?" I asked, but he'd already disappeared into the throng.

"Your input is duly noted, Widow Lucas," said the mayor, and I hoped that was the end of her input.

However, I knew better. "And you can note this too, Mr. Mayor," Granny continued, shouldering her way to get as close to him as possible. "If you allow the Forget-Me-Not ball to take place on the next full moon, as scheduled, the wolves will have one hell of a feast on our young people." A few villagers gasped, and others sniggered.

I waved my hand in the air, and the mayor acknowledged me with a nod. It seemed like every pair of eyes in the entire hall was glued on me, and my cheeks felt hot. Finally, I said, "Never mind."

"Sorry, dear, but you need to speak up," the mayor said. "Otherwise, we can't hear you."

I swallowed, and if my cheeks were red before, now they were on fire. I glanced at Granny, who was up on her toes and craning her neck to try and see me over the sea of people. Taking a deep breath, I faced the mayor and shouted, "What's the harm in rescheduling the ball for another night? One that isn't during Wolfstime?" I couldn't believe I'd spoken up, and with such confidence! While waiting for him to answer, I concentrated on not biting my lip.

The mayor hitched his belt and said, "I'm a firm believer that it's better to be safe than sorry. You, the fine people of this village, have made me your mayor, and I don't take my job, or your lives, lightly. After all, what good would it be to be your mayor if there's no one to preside over?" He chuckled to himself and then cleared his throat. "So, as requested by the Widow Lucas and her granddaughter, the Forget-Me-Not ball will be rescheduled for a safer date."

My eyes widened and I hid my smile behind my hand. I caught Granny's eye from across the town hall. Her hands were fisted to her side, and her lips were curled into a little smile. Though thirty-or-so folks were between us, it felt like we were standing side by side.

"But, Father, the hunters are going to kill the wolves tonight," Florence called out in her shrill voice, and I turned along with the other villagers to see her in the back of the room. "We have faith in our hunters to get the job done."

The young people around her pumped their fists in the air in agreement, shouting, "Kill the wolves!" and "It's our time! Nothing is going to take our special night away from us!"

With her arms crossed over her chest and a smug expression on her face, Violet looked like a statue standing in the midst of the commotion.

They quieted down when the mayor rang the bell. "I have faith in them as well," he said. "However, even if our courageous and competent hunters slay all the wolves they can, there is simply no way of knowing for sure whether or not they've eliminated the beast responsible for Amos Slade's demise. As Miss Lucas brought up, no harm will come from rescheduling the Forget-Me-Not ball so that it falls on a night that is not during Wolfstime."

"But the ball has always been held on the eve of the Flower Moon," said Violet. "It's one of the long-running traditions for our village. What will be next? Rescheduling Christmas for July?" Again, the young people voiced their support of her cause.

"If it means keeping our village safe, the answer is yes," said the mayor as he glanced down at the scroll. "Now, let's move on. It's come to my attention that many of you are disgruntled about the new fee being charged to market vendors. And here to inform us more about this new decree is Hershel Worthington, the royal tax collector."

Once Mr. Worthington took the stand, Peter nudged me, and I looked over to see Violet snaking her way through the people, headed straight for us. "She's not used to being shut down," he said.

"I think she's handling it quite well, actually," I said. "She looks rather becoming with a beet red face and steam blowing out of her ears, don't you think?"

Peter chuckled. "Speaking of beets, looks like the tax man's vegetable-dodging skills could use some work." Sure enough, there were smears of red, purple, and green on the back of his shirt. As soon as Violet sidled up to us, he stopped laughing and said, "Good show, Violet."

But she ignored him and leaned her face toward mine. "You and your grandmother have gone way too far," she said, her hands on her hips and her eyes ablaze. "The Forget-Me-Not ball is going to happen when it's supposed to, even if the mayor has forbidden it."

"Well, then, as my granny said, you'll be a bunch of dead idiots," I said calmly.

Violet frowned and stepped back. "Can't you see,

Red? It's nothing but a load of hype, meant to keep us quaking with false fear. The old fogies of this village want us to stay behind locked windows and doors—where they can keep close watch over us."

I had to admit, I was sick of being on lockdown, too. I was sick of the wolves terrorizing our village. I could only fantasize about a place where I could sleep peacefully at night, without having to make my home a fortress against the ferocious beasts. I longed to go someplace where I didn't have to look over my shoulder—where I could walk past a shadow, or hear a mysterious noise, and not have the little hairs on the back of my neck stand on end. A place I could go out to fetch the eggs and not have to fear that our chickens had been slaughtered. Most of all, I wanted to live someplace where I didn't have to constantly be afraid for my life or for the lives of my neighbors.

Maybe if I went in search of Lake Nostos, I would find such a place. Wait, what was I thinking? The whole notion of going on a quest for a fairy-tale lake was ridiculous. The wizard might have been a man of magical integrity once upon a time. After all, my own grandmother and mother went to him for magic. But who was to say he hadn't lost his marbles between then and now? And yet, if I never tried to find the lake, Granny would have to live with her pain for the rest of her years, and I couldn't bear to think that way.

"Come on, Violet. What about Mr. Slade?" Peter asked, patting the pitiable hound on its back. "That's not just some tale out of a storybook. It really happened. With our own eyes, we saw him lying in a pool of his own blood, surrounded by giant wolf tracks."

"He was a very old man," Violet said with a little shrug. "He split off from the hunting party, and he was too feeble to kill the wolf on his own. Or maybe he died of old age or a heart attack or something, and a wolf happened upon his old bones and made a midnight snack out of him. It's unpleasant and a bit on the bloody side, but it's life.

"We aren't like Amos Slade, though," Violet continued,

apparently unaware of the "Are you buying this?" looks Peter and I kept exchanging. And, in all honesty, I wished I could believe Violet's words. It would make our lives much simpler and the solution to our wolf problem more promising. "We are young. This is *our* time! And we are taking our lives back, starting tonight."

"What's tonight?" I dared to ask, a bad feeling forming in the pit of my stomach.

But she just put her finger to her lips and went back to join her friends.

I asked Peter, "Want to get out of here?" With a grin, he nodded and followed me, and his new hound dog brought up the rear.

Twenty-One

Peter and I sat at the edge of the swimming hole, dipping our bare toes into the cool bluish-green water while the hound dog snoozed in the shade. I was glad the hound was finally warming up to me a little, because whether Peter realized it or not, he had himself a dog now.

The music of the forest was a welcome change from the heated debates no doubt going on at town hall right about then. I closed my eyes to better hear the bees buzzing and the water lapping lazily against the rocks on the shoreline. When I caught the distinctly beautiful and haunting song of a nightingale, I sighed to myself. It was so nice to have them back in our part of the woods. I'd missed them all winter.

Suddenly, I recalled some of Knubbin's words: *Some say the truth rings as clear and sweet as a nightingale's song.* Maybe the wizard wasn't loony. Perhaps it was a riddle he meant for me to figure out, one that would help me find Lake Nostos. After all, didn't he say something about me having a lot to do before the birds migrate for the winter as I was leaving his—or whoever's it was—cabin yesterday? And in the age-old fairy tale about Lake Nostos, didn't the king tell his queen that he listened to the nightingales sing as he washed his face and hands in the cool waters of the spring?

"I should probably be getting back," Peter said—words that I was not happy to hear, even though I knew he was right. He grabbed our stockings and shoes from behind us, placing them within easy reach. "I'd rather stay here with you, but the meeting for the hunters will be starting any moment now. My father will wonder where I am."

"Are you afraid for tonight?" I asked once I'd tugged on my boots.

He scratched behind his ear. "Not afraid, really. Just

a bit nervous. I really hope one of us kills whatever it was that killed Amos Slade. I'd love to slay the wolves and free our village from their reign of terror, once and for all."

My gut roiled at the thought of Peter facing the monster. If a wolf sunk its deadly teeth and claws into my love, I might as well throw myself into the thick of Wolfstime without my cloak.

"I don't suppose I can talk you out of being in the hunting party," I said.

"Not a chance," he replied, just as I knew he would.

I scrambled to my feet and walked over to the tree on which I'd hung my cloak, bow, and quiver. He met me under the bough, and I handed him the silver-tipped arrow he'd made me. "Will you take this, this time? It would make me feel a lot better." I gave him what I hoped looked like a reassuring smile.

As he took the arrow, his fingers dragged from my wrist to my fingertips. The sensation took me by surprise, and it gave me a crop of goose bumps.

"Only if you take this," he said. He reached into his pocket and nonchalantly pulled out a gold cross necklace.

My jaw dropped in utter disbelief.

It was *my* gold cross necklace, the one that had been my mother's once upon a time. The one on which the wizard had put a spell, so that my mother could understand her Wolfstime dreams and, in time, realize her true self. The one I'd given to Hershel Worthington to pay off Granny's debt so we wouldn't lose the cottage.

"Peter . . ." I breathed.

"Turn around, and I'll put it on for you."

As I turned, my head kept spinning. "But . . . how?"

"Good ole Uncle Jenkins might be nothing more than a two-bit bandit, but he taught me a thing or two about pickpocketing."

Something fluttered within my belly. "Looks like we're both thieves. I can't believe you stole for me," I said, beaming at him.

"You'd better believe it. And hopefully, this time, you won't lose it or give it away. It's becoming a full-time job, just keeping it on you."

While Peter fastened the necklace around my neck, I caressed the smooth, familiar gold and smiled—until a terrible thought crossed my mind. "Oh, Peter! Mr. Worthington is going to give it to his wife. When he discovers it's missing, what if he comes after Granny again?"

"Ah, but I already thought of that. You see, I made you a cross pendant out of some scrap metal last night, before I went out with the hunting party. I knew how much the pendant meant to you, Red, and I knew that nothing, especially a replica made of copper, would truly be able to replace it. Still, I thought you might like to have something at least to remember it by. I meant to give it to you this morning, that's why I was headed to your house. But then, on my way, I heard you scream, and then there was Amos . . ."

"I know. So terrible," I said, trying to shake the tragic scene from my memory.

"Then, at the town hall, when I saw the tax man waving your mother's gold cross in front of your nose, something in me snapped. I knew I had to steal it from the bastard. I hated that he had something that's so special to you. I didn't know for sure if I could manage the whole switcheroo, but I figured I'd have the best shot while he was busy dodging rotten vegetables."

"Wait, you made me a cross pendant?" I asked, my heart melting as I turned back around and our eyes met.

"Sure did! A really good one, too. All it took was a bit of smithy magic. I'll be amazed if the tax man ever realizes it's not real gold. But if he does, we'll just have to figure something else out. Don't worry, Red. I won't let the tax man take your house."

"I can't believe you did all of that for me. You have a big heart, Peter."

He chuckled. "Well, if I'm being completely honest with you—part of the reason I did it was purely selfish."

"Oh?" I asked.

"I hoped my valiant—though arguably unlawful—act might earn me a kiss from the fairest maiden in the land." With a hint of a smile, he placed his hands on both sides of my head. Closing my eyes, I felt the warm sunlight on my face and the breeze in my hair.

He placed a kiss on my forehead and another on my nose. Though they were light as feathers, the kisses he trailed over my skin had an amazing way of stirring the very blood within my veins. When his lips moved to my cheek and then to the spot where my ear touched my neck, it felt oh, so wonderful—and yet, it made me greedy for more.

I inclined my head, my lips positively tingling in anticipation. When nothing happened right away, I peeked. Somehow, the way he was unabashedly staring at me with his beautiful brown eyes made me melt.

What if, when I tell him about the quest, he just laughs at me? What if he says he cannot come? Being apart from him would be unbearable.

"Here, sit down," Peter said. He sat on the log and patted the space beside him.

"But you have to go to the meeting, Peter."

"I know you want to tell me something. You look like you're about to explode. Why don't you just tell me, and then we'll head back to town."

I wedged my hands between my knees, hoping to

keep my legs from jittering so badly. "Remember when I told you I wanted to leave this village—that I wanted to go far, far away?"

Nodding, he said, "Of course I do. We'll go together, you and me." The dog gave a yelp, and Peter patted his head. "And we'll bring this bag of fleas, too, I guess."

I took a deep breath and blurted, "Granny has a very painful scar on her arm. I think I might have discovered something that can bring her relief."

"That's great, Red. What is it?"

"A drop of water from Lake Nostos."

He whispered, "Lake Nostos," to himself and then said, "I think I've heard of it, but I can't put my finger on it . . ."

"It's from the fairy tale about the washerwoman who was cursed to live in the water. Granny read it to us when we were children."

"Ah, that's right. A magical lake from a fairy tale." He arched his right eyebrow, and I could tell he was hoping I was only joking.

"I know it sounds crazy, and it probably is—all right,

it definitely is—but I want to see if I can find it," I said. "It will be my quest."

"And I suppose you want me to come with you on this quest?"

"Well, I was going to ask if I could borrow your horse. But you can come, too, if it makes you happy," I said with a little laugh. I scooted closer to him so that our legs touched.

"I already told you, walking around the Enchanted Forest with you is one of my favorite pastimes. So, when do we leave?"

"The sooner the better," I said. If the nightingales' song would help me find Lake Nostos, I needed to go before they migrated for the winter. Plus, there were, what, twenty-four days until the next Wolfstime, and it was always safest to travel when the wolves weren't hunting. I already had the money I'd saved, since Knubbin had returned it to me. "How about tomorrow night?"

Peter pinched the bridge of his nose and shook his head. "But Red, I can't leave the village. Not now. I have to help the hunters take down the wolves, and I have to help my father with the blacksmithing. They're counting on me. And people are counting on you, too. You have to help your grandmother with her deliveries. And who is going to put Violet in her place, if not you?"

I had to grin at his comment about Violet. And overall, his point was valid. However, if I didn't go in search of the final ingredient for the magic salve, no one would. Granny didn't know it, but she was counting on me. "I just want to help my granny," I said softly. "She's done so much for me, more than you know."

"You've done so much for her, as well. You saved her cottage from being seized by the king, and that's no small feat. I'm certain your granny is very grateful and very proud of you."

His words made my breath hitch. I hoped that Granny felt that way.

"What's the harm in waiting just a little longer, Red? Not forever, but just until things are better here in our village." He took my chin in his hand. "Don't go without me. Promise you'll wait for me."

Peter pulled me close and kissed me. He kissed me hungrily, and as our kiss deepened, I clenched the fabric of his sleeves, holding on for dear life with both hands. I straightened my posture, wanting even more of him, but he abruptly pulled away. His eyes flashed dangerously. "Promise me," he said again.

Once I could breathe again, I said, "All right, Peter. I'll wait."

"Good. I can only hope that I get to play a part in your happy ending, Red."

"Really?" I asked, wiping my tears. "I mean, I had a feeling . . . I really hoped it was true, I just . . ."

"Of *course* I do." He whirled around and kicked a rock so high and hard that it landed near the opposite shore of the pond. The dog snuffled and perked his ears, but he apparently didn't notice anything amiss, because he flopped back down and closed his eyes. "You're smart, beautiful, funny, and passionate—*and* you're the most skilled archer I know."

My heart fluttered in an unfamiliar way, and I was at

once overjoyed and nervous. "My granny is a much better shot than I am."

Peter shook his head and grinned. "That is not the point, Red." He closed the small distance between us and placed his hands on my shoulders. "What I'm trying to tell you—though you're making it awfully difficult for me—is that I love you."

I opened my mouth—in surprise rather than to say anything—but he pressed a finger against my lips and said, "Let me finish. I love that you're the *second best* archer I know. I love that you made me a birthday cake. Although, for my eighteenth birthday, you'd better bake me one that I actually get to eat. I love the wildness in your eyes and the kindness in your heart." He moved his finger from my lips to my hair, brushing a piece of it off my face. "I love that when you get something on your mind, the world had better watch out."

"Right now, you're the only one who needs to watch out," I said. I wrapped my hands around the back of his neck and pressed my lips against his.

"And I love the way you kiss me—" he murmured once we came up for air.

"Shhhhh," I said, and then kissed him all over again.

I felt like I was in a dream—but not a Wolfstime dream. In this one, everything around me seemed enhanced. As the sun set, the sky, the trees, and the flowers were extra vibrant, like a rainbow had fallen out of the sky and spilled over everything in the land. The ground felt springier and the sounds of nature more musical. Even in my bedroom, in the soft glow of my sconces and bedside candlesticks, the same old furnishings and decorations seemed extra beautiful.

I pressed my fingers to my lips, amazed how they still tingled. With a little help from my imagination, I could still feel all of the places Peter had set my bare skin on fire with his magical touch. He'd had to run from the swimming hole to town as fast as he could, and though he was a swift runner, there was no way he would've made it on time. I blushed a little as I wondered if the other hunters would be able to see our tryst written on his face.

I felt so different. Did I *look* different?

As I sat on the foot of my bed in my nightgown, brushing the tangles and a few small leaves out of my hair, I examined my reflection in the looking glass. My cheeks and lips had taken on a lovely shade of pink. Despite the tears I'd cried—or maybe because of them—my eyes were their brightest green. And, to answer my own question, I smiled at the glowing girl in my mirror and said, "Yes, you most definitely look different."

Moments later, my eye caught the reflection of the golden cross that dangled from my neck. It felt good to have it back where it belonged. Yet, on second thought, I hesitated to wear it on this last night of Wolfstime, for fear of it being the darkest nightmare I'd ever had. Why suffer through another frightful, fitful dream when I could possibly have a nice one? I unclasped the chain and let it slither into my open palm.

Then again, my mother hadn't seemed afraid of her Wolfstime dreams. She'd had Knubbin enchant the cross so that her Wolfstime dreams would expose her truest self. If she wasn't afraid, why was I?

As clearly as if someone were whispering them into my ear, I heard the words that I'd heard in my dreams: *"Only when you refuse to be a victim of fear will you know your true power."*

Twenty-Two

My feet sink into the mud, and with each step, the ground hardens—around my ankles, mid-calves, knees—making it more and more difficult to keep moving.

But I have to. I can't just stand still and allow the darkness to bury me alive.

Not tonight.

I reach up and out with all of my power, thrashing against an attack of dirt, branches, and rocks. I've lost my traction; it's all I can do to keep from slipping into the cavern that's yawning wider and wider below me. My legs dangle helplessly into the void, and my fingers sear and throb with pain as they grasp clusters of grass and roots.

I hear my heart pounding and the blood gushing through even the smallest of my veins. Then the voice wafts past my ears on a gust of air, and I remember to breathe. As I fill my lungs, the earth shifts, and I'm on all fours, crawling away from the hole. I can't tell if I've traveled a few seconds or a few days, but I'm making progress— until I hit my head against something hard. A beam of silvery light illuminates a large gray rock. I push, trying to move it. It won't budge; it's as if it's rooted deeply in the ground.

Then, as the clouds open up and release the moon, I gasp. It's not an ordinary rock; it is a gravestone—weathered and overgrown. I peel away the veil of vines, pricking my finger on a thorn. The shape of a crescent moon is carved into the stone. I trace my finger over the engraving, a strong sense of familiarity tugging at my soul.

A bloodcurdling scream slashes through the forest, making the hair on the back of my neck stand on end. Before I run, I look to the gravestone one last time. Under the moon's pale light, a single drop of blood glistens in the center of the crescent.

I woke with a start in my own bed, my fingers wrapped around my gold cross pendant. I felt winded and harried, and the mattress was clammy with perspiration. I'd been awake just long enough to allow my eyes to adjust to the candlelight and to gather my bearings.

Just another Wolfstime dream, I reminded myself, *and this should be the last one until the next full moon.*

I closed my eyes, trying to bring back as many details of my dream as possible. And that's when I heard it again—the bloodcurdling scream. Only it sounded so lifelike, I could have sworn somebody was actually screaming. My eyes popped open, and I jumped out of my bed. The same urge I'd had when I'd heard the frightening sound in my nightmare stormed through my blood: the need to run.

After checking that Granny was safe, sleeping in her usual Wolfstime post, I took my red riding hood, bow, and quiver and raced into the deep, dark forest. Though mist shrouded the moon, I could somehow see as well as if it were midday. Energy and power coursed through my body as I tore through the branches and hurtled the logs, bushes, and rocks. I heard the cries again—louder and more desperate—and though it made no sense that I could hear the screams from so far away, I knew in my gut that they were coming from the clearing where Peter's birthday party had been.

Peter! Was he all right?

Speeding up, I had no sensation of my feet hitting the ground, only the wind ripping around me. The moon-light intensified and faded as its cloud cover drifted, and though the moment felt surreal, it also felt meaningful—like it was all somehow part of my destiny.

A dying bonfire flickered and smoked as people scattered into the woods, some wailing, others sobbing. Beatrice was bent over something on the ground, rocking back and forth miserably. When she shifted slightly to look at me, I saw that it was Florence lying there, her red curls splayed out around her, her eyes closed.

"Red!" Beatrice cried out. "Watch out! The wolf! It's here."

"Is Florence . . . ?" My voice stuck in my throat.

"No, no. She's going to be all right. She fainted when she saw the wolf," she said, and relief washed over me. "It's horrible, Red! It's even more horrible than your granny said it was! It's huge—the biggest wolf I've ever seen—and it has these terrible yellow eyes that glow in the dark. And now, now it's after Violet!" She pointed to the tree behind which I'd hidden the last time I was there.

The wind shifted direction, bringing with it Violet's honeysuckle scent. I reached in my quiver for an arrow, surprised to see the shining silver tip. *Oh, no! If I have the silver-tipped arrow that means Peter slipped it back into my quiver. Which means Peter is out there hunting the wolves without it!* I swallowed hard and rolled back my shoulders as I ran toward the tree.

Violet leaned against a giant tree trunk, slowly sinking to the ground as her knees buckled beneath her. On a knoll ten feet in front of her loomed the wolf.

It was enormous, at least three times the size of any

wolf I'd ever seen. Long gray fur stuck up on its back, and its snout wrinkled menacingly. It pulled back its lips and let out a low growl that seemed to reach out and seize my heart. Each of its gleaming razor-sharp teeth was larger than one of my hands! It was as if the creature didn't belong in this realm at all, but rather someplace far away, where wolves were bigger, more ferocious, and deadlier.

I had no doubt that this was the monster that had murdered Amos Slade, and that it wouldn't stop with him. It acknowledged my presence with a twitch of its ear, yet it kept its wild, amber-colored eyes trained on Violet.

Fear paralyzed me, yet somehow I managed to pull back my bow and take a step toward Violet. She let out a scream when the wolf lunged forward and a strained whimper when it froze about four feet from us. It was close, much too close. I cringed at the stench of blood on its warm, steady breath. It reached out its enormous paws and stretched out its claws, reaching for Violet. Its fangs seemed to grow before my terrified eyes.

My eyelids twitched, wanting to shut out the horror, but I forced myself to stare at it. "Don't even think about it, wolf," I said with as much confidence as I could muster.

Keeping the silver-tipped arrow aimed at the beast's heart, I knelt next to Violet and told her, "Get under my cloak. It will protect us. You must believe." She huddled against me as I draped the cloak over her body. Her trembles shook me until I couldn't tell the difference between hers and mine.

The clouds parted and set free the Wolfstime moon, as full and bright as the one in my dreams. For the first time, the wolf's amber eyes met mine. It was as if they were lit from inside by torches. Spellbound, I couldn't look away. I didn't dare breathe.

My heart beat strong and hard, sending my blood gushing through my veins. From somewhere deep inside, I heard the voice from my Wolfstime dreams, reminding me to breathe. I inhaled deeply. As I exhaled, I felt the air leave my body and flow out into the night, becoming one with the world.

In that instant, in the brilliant moonlight, I let my arrow fly.

Time seemed to stand still, and I wondered if I'd somehow missed. Then the wolf took two steps forward. It bowed its mighty head and fell over on its side with a cloud of dust and a terrible thud. Its eyelids slowly lowered as if it were being lulled to sleep. Before they closed, I saw that the glow was gone from its eyes.

As I lowered my weapon, I heard shouts and glimpsed flashes of fire. I had to blink twice to make sure my mind wasn't playing tricks on me when I saw Peter and the hound behind us, running up the knoll.

"Red! Red, are you all right?" Peter asked, and he rushed over to me while the dog took refuge behind a bush. "We heard the screams, and when we got to the clearing, Beatrice told me you'd gone after the wolf!" His handsome face was wrought with concern as he looked me over.

Violet came out from under my cloak. "She did," she said, her big brown eyes glistening with tears. "And she saved my life." She pointed straight ahead, and Peter held up his torch, illuminating the wolf's lifeless body.

Peter's jaw slacked open. He handed his torch to Violet and, with a death grip on his bow, cautiously approached the beast. "I've never seen anything like it," he said breathlessly. "It's . . . enormous."

"It's dead, right?" I asked.

Peter nodded. "Red, you slayed the wolf. Straight through the heart. It was a perfect shot," he said as he pulled out the arrow. He handed it to me. The blood-covered silver tip shone brilliantly in the moonlight.

I knew it made no sense for me to cry. I should be happy the wolf was dead. However, as soon as Violet headed up the road to her house, assuring me that she'd have her father and the other hunters go back for the wolf's body, warm tears spilled down my face. I felt Peter's hand around mine, holding on until we saw the lights of my home. He stopped on the trail, as always.

"Walk me all the way home, Peter."

"You sure?" he asked, and I nodded and took his hand again.

We crossed the path, and he held the torch high to light up the stairs as we climbed them. I took a breath and smiled. "It's going to be all right," I said, more to myself than him. "Everything is going to be all right." Then I knocked on the door, shouting for Granny to let us in.

We heard the banging and sliding of wood on metal and, finally, the door swung open. Granny's gray hair fell long and wild past her shoulders, and her cheeks were flushed. She cinched the belt on her robe as she glowered at the pair of us. "What in the land—?"

"Red killed the wolf," Peter said, skipping all small talk.

I held up the silver-tipped arrow for her to see. She looked at him and next at me. Then she took the arrow and ran her finger over the blood-stained tip. "Can it be so?"

I nodded. "It's dead, Granny."

She blinked several times, and finally pushed the door open wider. "Well, don't just stand out there like a couple of idiots." After we filed inside, she shut the door behind us. "I'm going to get dressed. I'm sure our guest would like some cider. Will you see to that, Red?"

"Oh, yes, of course," I stammered. "Coming right up." Maybe if I hurried, Granny wouldn't scare Peter off.

While I filled the kettle, I gazed out the little kitchen window. In the western sky, I spotted the pale, full moon for a mere second before it faded into the horizon, not to be seen until the next Wolfstime. The sun began to rise, its yellow-orange glow reminding me of the wolf's eyes. There had been so much mystery in those eyes.

Soon after, Peter poked his handsome head in the kitchen and grinned. For having been alone with my grandmother, I couldn't help noticing that he appeared awfully merry. "*Hallo*, Red. There's quite a crowd out here, and they're all asking for you. Looks like my sweetheart is a hero."

He called me his *sweetheart*. For a second or two,

I melted like a pat of butter in a hot skillet. But then Granny showed up right behind him—thankfully in her clothes, now—and I felt certain she'd overheard. I steeled myself for having to deal with her wrath.

I wanted Granny to understand how wonderful Peter was, and to help her see that I loved him. Deep inside, I longed for her to know those truths about me. I wanted her to accept Peter. I wanted her to accept me.

But oddly, and thankfully, Granny was grinning. She whisked past Peter and started unwrapping baked goods and arranging them on plates. "Well, what are you waiting for, child? Get out there!"

Peter shepherded me out to the living room where, sure enough, a crowd of villagers waited—and more were arriving. Mayor Filbert stepped forward and patted my shoulder. "Here she is, folks. The heroine who saved the life of young Violet Roberts." The thunder of applause filled the little cottage.

I didn't have a chance to respond before Violet's mother pushed through the throng. With tears in her eyes, she squeezed my hand and said, "You are a very brave young lady. We cannot thank you enough, Red."

Beatrice came over next, thanking me in between bites of one of Granny's muffins. Granny and Peter were already circulating through the crowd, handing out baked treats. Florence still looked pale and haggard, and yet she hugged me with surprising strength.

With her tangled locks and dirty, torn skirt, Violet appeared shabbier and more pitiful than I'd ever fathomed possible, even in my most spiteful daydreams. "I was wrong about you, Red," she said, loud enough for our classmates to hear. "I'm glad we're friends now."

I smiled beatifically at her. "Yes, you were most definitely wrong about me."

A few minutes later, Peter brought me a drink and said something about taking his hound to the stream for some water.

"You know, you're going to have to name that dog someday," I said.

"Already have. His name is Copper. I thought of it when I was making the new cross pendant for you."

I smiled. "I like it. It suits him."

Peter slipped out, and the others gathered around me, thanking me and talking about how brave I was. I grinned until my cheeks ached, but after a little while longer, I felt suffocated by all the people and all the attention. I searched for Peter and found him outside on the rope swing.

"So, when I was in the kitchen, you called me something you've never called me," I prompted, pulling the swing toward me and then giving him a hearty push.

"A hero," he said.

"No, something else . . ."

He dragged his boot in the dirt, slowing to a near stop. After he wiped a tendril of hair off my cheek, he eased me onto his lap. "Sweetheart," he said.

I leaned back, melding into him. "Yes, that's it," I whispered.

The front door swung open, and Granny hollered, "Red, get back in here, now. I need some help keeping all these folks properly fed." She wagged her finger at Peter. "And as for you, you wastrel, there will be no hanky-panky with my granddaughter, you hear me?"

"Yes, ma'am," Peter said, helping me off his lap.

I sighed and shrugged. "Sorry."

"It's all right," he said, chuckling softly. "She's not nearly as ruthless as my brothers. Go."

My brief tryst with Peter gave me the boost I needed to dive back into the bustling cottage. I hadn't even made it to the kitchen to fill a tray with refreshments when a loud rap sounded on the front door. Granny opened it, and when I craned my neck, I saw Violet's father and a group of men standing on the porch, long-faced and wide-eyed.

"We went where Violet told us the wolf was," Mr. Roberts said, "and we could tell precisely where it fell. But the body . . . it's gone."

Peter pushed through the men. "What are you saying? How can that be possible?"

"Someone must have gotten to it before us," Peter's father said, holding his palms up.

I started making my way toward Granny and Peter,

but an eerie sound stopped me in my tracks. The world around me seemed to stand still and silent, except for a faint echo. With a shudder, I met Granny's eyes across the room, and I knew in my heart that she'd heard it, too.

It was the howl of a lone wolf.